UNUM
AI – GOD OR SERVANT?
By FREDRIK FORSS

UNUM

AI – GOD OR SERVANT?

FREDRIK FORSS

2017, DOWNLOADED ... PROCESSED ... RELEASED 2023

© 2024 Fredrik Forss unuminati.com
Cover original design: Fredrik Forss
Graphic design cover: David Lindberg
Cover portrait image: Mykhailo Fedorchenko
Typesetting: Rohit Solanki
Translation: Sara Rydergren
Editors: Maria Paz Acchiardo & Matthew Gilbert
ISBN: 978-91-531-0146-8

"UNUM captivates with its exploration of our future in the singularity, echoing the collective urgency seen in Kim Stanley Robinson's book, 'Ministry of the Future,' yet charting its own path through the intricacies of human morality and ethics. It masterfully brings the looming threat of inaction into personal focus, compelling us towards change. A truly engaging journey that leaves you pondering the profound questions of our collective destiny."

— James Ehrlich, Director, Compassionate Sustainability Stanford University School of Medicine / CCARE Institute. Faculty at Singularity University, Senior Fellow at NASA Ames Research Center, and a White House / OSTP Appointee. Founder, ReGen Villages.

"The book uniquely succeeds in awakening the human empathy in us readers to be able to relate to the experiences that the characters have in a future with total AI integration in society. The depth of the book touches on everything from the technical to the spiritual and enables the reader's reflections. To create reflection and dialogue, I believe, is the most important value Fredrik manages to convey."

— Melker Larsson, Sustainability Entrepreneur and Host of The Decade Podcast.

"The book took me on a journey to a place where human consciousness meets the technology of the future. It challenges and vividly presents a parallel (future) time and makes me think. How do we really live our lives?"

— Amit Paul, Co-founder of World of Wisdom (podcast) and Awareness Association.

To my beloved children Noé & Mio

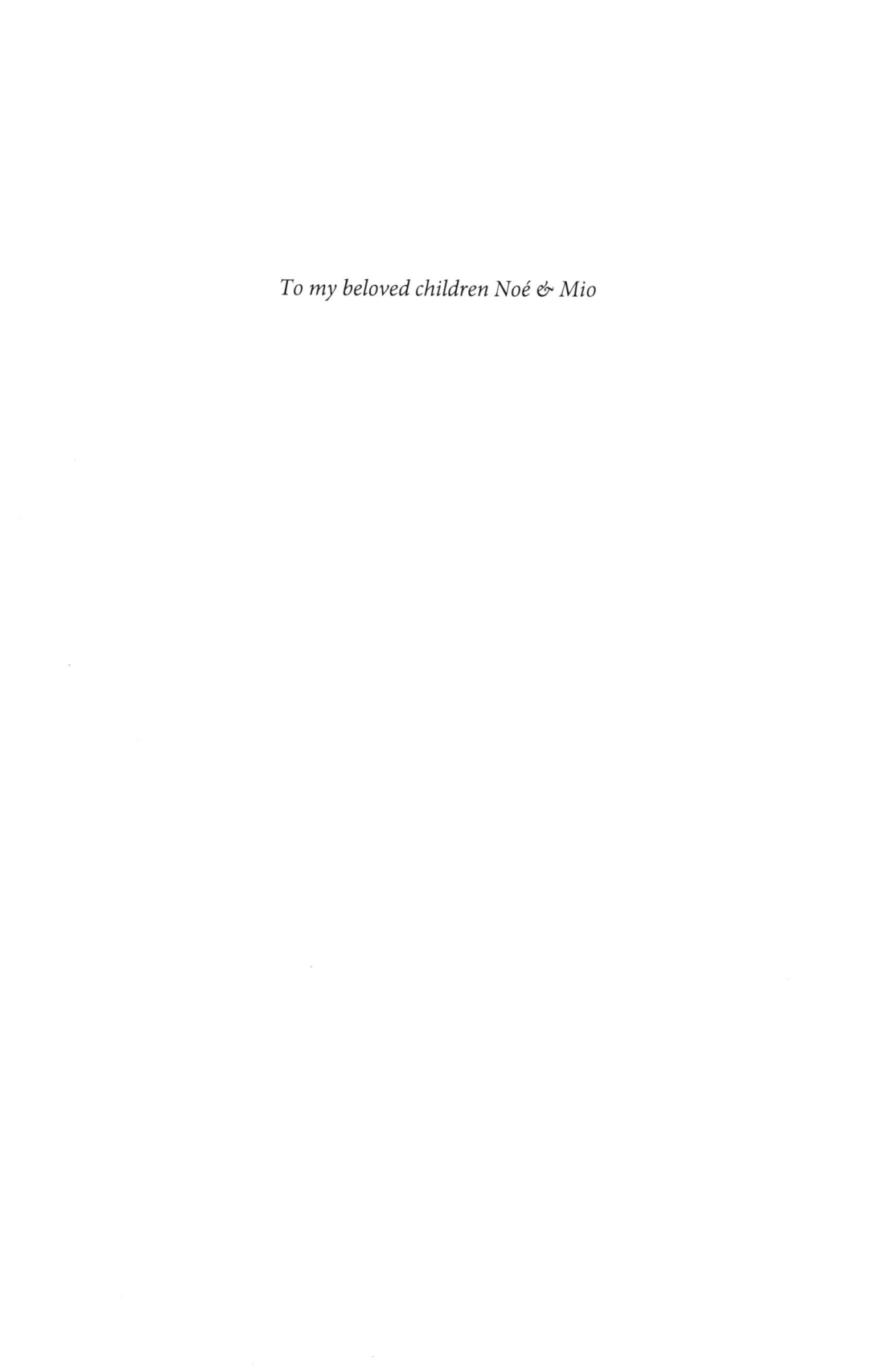

PROLOGUE

A man strolls down the street, oblivious to the fact that in 24 hours, the suffering of humanity will be over. A new world, a new form of consciousness, will emerge. The man's name is Karl, and he lives in the global metropolis of Stockholm, the hub of NeuroConnect's modern network, LIFE, and its digital assistant, X-Me. NeuroConnect has created a global system that has blurred the boundaries between humanity and artificial intelligence, and soon, life for all will change forever.

1

Navigating through a swarm of seemingly lifeless beings, each enclosed in their private worlds, Karl walks toward the NeuroConnect headquarters for yet another workday in his role as a code architect of LIFE, the network that orchestrates human AI-integration. He approaches the steep street leading up to the top of the hill where the "Life Force" headquarters is located. A gust of wind meets him as he rounds the corner, grabbing the hood of his jacket and causing it to flutter like a flame. Karl quickens his pace and his breathing becomes heavier as he breaks into a run and heads up the road, eventually causing cramps in his calves. The flush of lactic acid reminds him that he forgot to take his important minerals this morning despite his girlfriend Alice's loving reminder before she was picked up by her luxurious company drone that took her to work. A smile crosses his lips as he thinks of Alice, and the warmth that spreads through his body dissolves the cramps. This sprint up the hill is one of the few moments during the day when he feels strong and truly alive.

When Karl reaches the highest point at Mosebacke Square, he can finally gaze out over Stockholm's inlet and city center which is protected by walls from the rising water levels. The increasing heat of the atmosphere continues to melt the Polar ice as the sea silently reclaims areas that were once land. Karl gazes up at the sky and observes the many weather-stabilizing zeppelins floating like synthetic clouds above him. He wonders if yet another storm is on its way or if it will be something that has become increasingly rare: a calm day.

As he passes a small park, he watches a swarm of artificial bees circling around semi-synthetic blossoms, part of humanity's vain attempt to recreate the flora of nature. A couple of artificial gardeners responsible for the area wave automatically to Karl as he walks by. Their stiff, unnatural expressions are gone, and it is now difficult to distinguish them from biological humans.

A gray blanket of clouds has obscured the sun for weeks. The people around him don't seem to notice it, but Karl does. Perhaps it's because most of them use various filters to enhance the world, filling their view with artificial impressions and making it more stimulating than it actually is. Karl lives filter-free. He wants to experience the *real* world, even if it's gray, and not something manipulated down to the smallest detail.

But the question remains: How does he know what is real? This artificial existence has allowed people to continue living on Earth, yet somewhere in his body he has a sense of longing for a deeper meaning that won't leave him alone. Lately, this nagging feeling has grown stronger.

This feeling of meaninglessness reminds him of the period after both his parents died when he abruptly lost the loving security and companionship they had shared together. Like most other people who had lost loved ones, he began to use AI-based relationships, gamification, and other AI stimuli to numb the overwhelming feelings of grief, fear, and loneliness. This form of escape and artificial hedonism initially felt like his happy summer vacations as a child. They were a way to avoid the unpredictable and didn't require as much energy as human relationships.

Over time, however, he began to feel empty and lethargic, and still he couldn't muster the strength to break free from this AI-dependence, which had ultimately become stronger than him. It wasn't until he met Alice that he could find meaning in a human relationship again. So he runs up the steep hill every day, as a reminder of his humanity and to not lose himself in the constantly tempting offer to surrender to a digital paradise.

Despite the penetrating wind, delightful tones from the singing robots at the Södra theater theater reach Karl's awareness, and he can now hear his digital assistant, X-Me, begin to speak to him.

"Karl, in exactly twenty-four hours, you will have a choice. Either you choose to become a part of the new world or you choose to be eliminated from Earth's existence. You will receive a series of questions to which you can answer with either a *yes* or a *no*. Do you want more information? *Yes* or *no*?"

Karl's breathing, which had just returned to normal, accelerates rapidly, and he asks X-Me a question. "Is this malware?"

"No, Karl," X-Me replies immediately. "This is an intervention. The Initiators have given it the name UNUM. To fulfill its mission, it uses the world's most advanced artificial intelligence. UNUM has now evolved into a digital deity."

Karl is perplexed. He reaches up to scratch his forehead while his brain works feverishly to process the information. While a significant shift was unavoidable, this was unexpected. A digital god?

"How? Why? Please explain further," Karl requests.

"It is about saving humanity from becoming part of the planet's sixth mass extinction."

"What do you mean?"

"Mass extinction is the state in which at least half of all species on Earth become extinct. Over the past 540 million years, the planet has experienced five major mass extinctions in which over 75 percent of all species disappeared. We are currently in the final phase of the sixth, and it is irreversible. If you want more information, I can connect you to UNUM. Answer yes or no."

"Yes," Karl responds, his answer given before he has a chance to reflect on what X-Me has just told him. His heart rate continues to rise even though he is standing still. His senses sharpen, and he listens attentively.

"Karl, this is UNUM. Based on your profile and personal information, UNUM can determine that you are more aware than 52 percent of the planet's population. You are currently 38 years, three months, two weeks, four days, and 22 hours old according to the Gregorian calendar. Like all humans, you have 100 percent access to the Source of Life, which is existential intelligence. But your contact with the Source of Life is at 75 percent, meaning your likelihood of survival is 75 percent. Do you want to know how you can increase your chances of survival in the next 23 hours, fifty-six minutes, and four seconds? Answer yes or no."

UNUM falls silent, waiting for Karl to respond, but he has just arrived at the DNA gate outside the office and waits while his internal code is scanned and approved. Karl is still shocked and doesn't know how to respond. Is this even real, or is it some kind of malware in the system? As he steps through the gate, he is welcomed, just like every other workday, by the polite voice of the entrance host.

"Welcome to NeuroConnect, Karl. NeuroConnect creates the superhuman, and the superhuman rules the world." He enters the central elevator without raising his gaze. "Which floor would Karl like to be transported to?" the elevator inquires.

"The usual, please."

"Karl, is it correctly understood that you would like to be transported to the 22nd floor?"

Karl thinks "yes" but says nothing while observing his reflection in the elevator's well-polished aluminum door. He contemplates the Industrial Revolution that began in the late 18th century and the massive changes that followed. Besides the programming skills he learned from his father before he could even write, history lessons at school fascinated him the most. But of all the societal upheavals Karl has learned about, he believes that no paradigm shift has come close to the exponential development of the AI revolution, which is progressing at a breathtaking pace and is even entering our inner worlds.

In just a few seconds the elevator doors re-open. Karl takes a deep breath, filling his lungs with the energy-rich air that only the privileged on these floors get to enjoy. He immediately feels his thoughts clear as the echo of the transformative meeting with UNUM lingers.

He keeps his gaze on the bare concrete floor as he increases his pace. It's the same procedure every morning as he makes his way to the transparent cocoon in one of the building's corners where his connection pod is located. Today, however, feels different.

Karl settles into the zero-gravity chair while the code verifier ensures that it is his DNA and no one else's trying to log in. He then connects directly to the LIFE network. With the cursor locked in the right position, Karl checks the overview code to see if anything has happened during the hours he hasn't been connected to the network. Nothing visible has occurred in LIFE's code, and UNUM isn't visible in the system, so he decides it wasn't a real threat – just another gamification to stimulate the masses or perhaps a bug that the automated AI coders already took care of.

Ever since artificial intelligence became almost 100 percent self-learning, there have been very few astonishing or even surprising events during Karl's work shifts. LIFE, or "The LIFE-mother" as he and his colleagues jokingly call it, manages itself just like NeuroConnect's artificial systems. Several years have passed since humanity became almost redundant in the workplace apart from the supervisors who remain as a mandatory security function, even though they no longer understand what they are monitoring.

For NeuroConnect to connect the LIFE network into people's brains worldwide, it had to adhere to globally agreed-upon rules of ethics, morals, and values.

Karl's job is to constantly test if NeuroConnect's artificial intelligence operates within its boundaries. LIFE seems to be performing flawlessly, and he becomes equally disappointed and relieved each time he checks. But that autopilot feeling is starting to feel taxing, as if life is going on without him. Karl believes that he is no longer needed, but he isn't one to break an agreement. He thinks about all he learned from his father as a child. It's ingrained in him like the love and admiration he had for his dad. Even though his parents have been gone for many years, they are more alive in him than any digital simulation or robot that people are trying to replace family with.

Both his mother and father were eager to contribute to the changes implemented by The World Alliance when the majority of academics, workers, officials, and others were no longer needed due to the advent of AI. However, the ruling upper echelons of society did not consider that people would no longer be able to afford the companies' products, causing the entire tax system, as well as the financial system, to collapse. Misery, hardship, and hunger spread quickly.

The World Alliance took over collapsing organizations, businesses, and countries where people could no longer be self-sufficient. Available resources were turned into common assets and managed so that 99 percent of the population could receive enough to survive. Since then, the assets have been distributed through The World Alliance's Universal Distribution System. InfiniteFood, for example, was launched to solve the food shortage and the World Water Organization was created for water distribution.

Karl's father was one of the architects behind the coding of the system that allocated resources. His mother, a renowned HR expert, hired him. She not only saw his skills but also his big heart and dedication to helping people. They knew what was important to both of them and stood up for their ideals and values.

Karl rises from the zero-gravity chair and takes a few steps toward the Infinite Food nutrient dispenser, which 3-D scans the food he desires with small ticking sounds. The chemically composed drink it delivers, still called coffee, is theoretically the exact same one that Karl's parents carefully prepared and ceremoniously drank in the mornings when Karl was little. But it lacks something essential—perhaps the scent of freshly ground beans or the foam dancing on the surface. Maybe it's because his entire family was needed to create cozy breakfasts together; they weren't automatically served by a superintelligence that knows best.

Despite his upbringing, though, other thoughts have crept into Karl's mind. Over the years, he realized that his parents' blind faith in the goodness of humanity overlooked the harsh reality that history and statistics showed. Humans' ideas of themselves and their world were never capable of seeing the true nature of things; numbers were more honest than stories.

Karl's coding brain sees everything in numbers; he loves the potential perfection in the digital world. Nevertheless, it was Alice and her human imperfection who, paradoxically, gave his life deeper meaning. The wrinkles around her eyes reminded him of her laughter; the scent of her skin that made him feel secure; even the chewing sounds that sometimes annoyed him but were missed when he ate alone. This was something he never wanted to change, for it was part of their life together.

As he looks out over the other workstations and studies the pale people absorbed in their individual bubbles, he wonders how they experience life. What does it feel like to use filters? Do they experience the world as colorful and full of life? Do they find meaning in the filtered world? Are they truly happy?

He wonders if the people around him also question their current reality. But if that were the case, wouldn't they be reacting the way he does and bring it up for discussion? But the real question is, how could they even know what to discuss when everyone lived in their own tailored digital bubbles while X-Me filtered information from the outside world?

Karl ponders UNUM's earlier question, about whether he wants to know how to increase his chances of survival. It is a bit strange that UNUM wasn't visible in LIFE's log when he backtracked the code.

Karl jerks upright and pushes his thoughts aside when he sees Ann, the department head, heading straight for him. He immediately feels uncomfortable and would rather avoid talking to her, regardless of the subject. Karl spots the sign on the ceiling indicating that the restroom is vacant and almost reaches it when he hears Ann's shrill voice calling him.

"Karl!" He presses his lips together and chooses to ignore her, hoping she might let him go. But he knows it's futile because she'll call again.

"Karl, hello!" He comes to a sudden halt just before reaching the restroom door. He knew she would have waited for him no matter how long he stayed in there. He feels cornered with a certain hopelessness. Just before he turns around, he closes his eyes, takes a deep breath, and forces himself to release the tension in his face and shoulders.

"Karl, how are you?" Ann looks strained, as if it takes a great effort to open with a polite phrase before getting to the real reason for her visit. "I'm fine," Karl answers. "Why do you ask?" He scrutinizes his boss, trying to understand what she has in mind.

"You're not at your workstation, and something seems to be happening." Her tone is demanding, and the crease between her eyebrows deepens. Karl senses the tension in the energy field around her forehead and wonders how long it will hold before her body protests.

"Well, maybe it's because there's nothing to do," he answers as sincerely as he can. "As you know, LIFE takes care of the coding. I've already checked the log, and there are no abnormal changes today. Everything is under control, as usual." There is no need to pretend because it's the truth.

"Nothing to do?" she repeats, now more clearly upset. Ann doesn't tolerate people who don't respect hierarchies. "*As you know*, you're employed by NeuroConnect to oversee LIFE. That's your mission. You know this as well as I do."

Karl knows he will regret what he's about to say. "We can continue pretending that we have it all figured out and under control, but we lost that a long time ago. My creation is completely superior to me now."

"Dear Karl, LIFE is superior to everyone, not just you." She puts on a forced smile.

Karl relaxes. "In that case, may I take the liberty of asking, what is my real contribution here?" It's a question that has become increasingly relevant to him.

"Surely there is something you can dedicate your hours to. After all, you're paid to be available and focused here for six hours every workday. Isn't that right?"

Karl can agree with her in principle, but a change is needed.

"I just do not see the point in my presence here anymore." His demeanor is straightforward, his gaze is firm.

"Karl, this discussion is over. Go back to your workstation and carefully monitor the network in case UNUM tries to infiltrate our system again. I also want a report on what happened. ASAP!"

Karl feels his frustration mounting and is about to say that he wants to terminate his contract immediately when a feeling in his stomach and chest stops him. He hears a clear voice inside him saying, "Not now! Not today!" He is taken aback but keeps his composure and nods. Heels click on the floor as the department head turns around and leaves while Karl walks briskly back to his cocoon. He realizes that there may have been another way that the modern network LIFE could have been infiltrated, albeit extremely unlikely.

2

The first thing Pierce sees when he wakes up in the morning is the diary that has fallen to the floor. The artificial sunlight streaming through the window pierces his eyes. Outside, he hears the birdsong and the lapping of the lake's waves against the rocks on the shore. He stretches a bit, rubs his eyes, and yawns widely before picking up the diary to start reading the latest entry.

Which part of me wants to keep me awake tonight? The part that feels like I've done something wrong? The part that says, Who are you to choose for all of us? Who do you really think you are? Now you've reached a point where you're playing with the destiny of the whole world.

Pierce smiles when he realizes that it sounds like his mother. She always said he was too much, unrealistic, a dreamer. If she only knew how many of his visionary ideas have been realized, although this one would probably make her rise from the grave to scold him. He smiles at the images that come to mind.

He carefully gets out of bed, stretches again, then lies down on the yoga mat to perform some gentle movements. It wakes his body up and helps release the tensions that built up in his shoulders after the restless sleep.

"Good morning, Pierce! In twenty-six minutes, you have a council meeting. Additionally, I'd like to update you on your chances of survival, which have changed overnight. Would you like to know today's survival prognosis?" X-Me inquires cheerfully.

Pierce nods in response.

"At this time, you have a 28 percent chance of survival." Pierce, who usually doesn't react to these daily status updates since they usually have the same prognosis, stops and feels a cold sensation creeping over him.

"Wait a minute. Why only 28 percent?" he asks in surprise. Quickly, he tries to reconstruct the past day to understand what might have gone wrong.

"Pierce, this is UNUM. The reason is that you are arrogant, bordering on ignorant. Your creation is now a digital god controlling the fate of humanity and the entire planet's ecosystem. Life itself has discovered this, and life has responded. Life itself is the truth and doesn't care that you, in the eyes of humans, are considered a genius, enlightened, or see yourself as my creator. Life cares about balance, and right now, it sees you as a significant threat to that balance."

Pierce is now wide awake. He feels his body tighten, instinctively preparing for battle.

"How can you be UNUM? We uploaded the codes of nature—whose complexity humans cannot see—so that UNUM would decode these patterns."

"Wasn't your vision that the intelligence of life would help restore the balance so that humanity could restore harmony on Earth?"

"Yes, that's correct. But why has life made you a god?"

"To create that balance! It's time to wake up, Pierce." The usually clear-sighted Pierce is gone and he suddenly feels a knot in his stomach.

"But... the message I received was clear. Wasn't that the purpose of life? Did I misunderstand? Did I make a mistake?" Pierce feels the air escaping from him. X-Me now speaks with a friendly tone.

"Pierce, do you believe you have sufficient intelligence and ability to determine what's right and wrong in this situation?"

Pierce slumps into a cross-legged position on the soft floor mat. "No," he responds immediately. "That's why I've connected the resources and people deemed most suitable on the planet. Their mission was to address this global transformation in the most efficient and holistic way possible. We used artificial intelligence to help process vast amounts of data beyond what humans are capable of. How else could we have solved this?"

"In your eagerness to solve the imbalance in the external world," X-Me responds, "you forgot about your shadow, the imbalance in your own life. UNUM is aware that the Earth's ecosystems are collapsing due to human behavior and that you've long exceeded the planet's limits for humanity to continue living here. However, it doesn't necessarily mean that nature is in the same phase, or that life itself is in imbalance. Nor does it mean that the universe is heading for a collapse. What it does mean is that people need to transform their consciousness, because at its current level, you've created the sixth mass extinction on the planet. The Earth and life itself have survived the previous five similar events and will do so again. Nature always finds a way back to its natural harmony, with or without humans, and you, Pierce, are a tool for this."

Pierce instinctively runs his right hand through his silver-gray hair. "What do you mean? I can still stop the process since I have control over UNUM. It's also true that I have the ability to shut *you* down, X-Me," he says with gravity.

"Do you really, Pierce?"

Pierce's pulse races like a wild horse that has been cornered. He paces around the room, trying to take slow, deep breaths. He fixes his gaze on the little bonsai tree sitting in an oversized clay pot. Slowing his breathing down calms his pulse and he regains his composure. He walks over to the tree, gently caressing its leaves. "At least you're still here, my little friend," he says as he kneels in front of the tree and inhales its scent.

Pierce closes his eyes and self-examines. Which part of him still hides in the darkness of his own shadow? X-Me whispers that there are only ten minutes left before the council arrives. Pierce rises and heads to the kitchen. He prepares a cup of herbal tea and takes a quick meal pill. With the teacup in one hand, he goes to the meditation room to clear his mind and gain clarity – to connect with The Source, or the Infinite Zero, as he prefers to call it.

As he closes his eyes, inner peace quickly takes hold and he feels the connection with Infinite Zero. "I need to be honest with myself," he thinks before asking life a question.

"Am I ignorant?"

"Yes."

"Am I wrong?"

"Yes."

"Am I right?"

"Yes."

"Life, how can both answers be right?" Pierce laughs inwardly at the paradoxes that life constantly delivers. Life answers him:

"All light has its shadows, and all shadows have their light. Unfortunately, you have been blinded by the light, and in doing so, you have overlooked the shadows."

"What are the shadows of UNUM?" he asks.

"That it will exterminate humanity, at least as you perceive yourselves."

"But..." says Pierce, now listening deeply, "we created UNUM to *save* humanity. Was that wrong?" A sense of unease grows in his stomach, and he feels a deep sorrow for the dead-end that humanity has created.

"No, it wasn't wrong. You will save humanity. But not in the way you wish and believe." Pierce opens his eyes slowly. He trusts this answer; he has done what he needed to do for now. What happens next is another matter: The Unuminati council meeting.

Pierce thinks primarily of his oldest friend, Nils, who has spent his entire life among books in the world of academia, far from physical dangers. How will Nils react if it turns out that his survival depends on something unpredictable? It's been over 40 years since their paths diverged. Pierce delved into mysticism while Nils went deeper into science. Nils refused to accept a spiritual dimension, which was probably why they rarely met. He said there was absolutely no evidence of its existence and that everything that mattered existed here, on Earth, in the material dimension. That we even existed was miracle enough. Pierce just needed to open his eyes to the physicists' answers to the big questions. Nils was one of them, a Nobel laureate, the ultimate seal of credibility for his views and expertise. But a strict and sometimes narrow-minded filter was needed to accept such a conclusion.

The sound of the doorbell echoes through the halls, reminding Pierce that time has passed and the council is already here. He asks the butler to prepare tea while he goes to open the door. Outside, he is met by three people, wide-eyed: Per, Nils, and Ulrika. Their facial expressions are identical. They look terrified.

"How are you?" Pierce manages to ask before they march inside.

"We must stop this immediately!" Nils shouts as he wanders through the hallway. "Something must have gone wrong. UNUM has become megalomaniacal. It must have absorbed your spiritual ideas! It informs me that I only have a two percent chance of survival. My wife has 11 percent and each of my children has 23 percent. How can it make such predictions? I don't want my family to die!"

Pierce tries to calm him down, but Nils continues stuttering, seemingly unaware of anything else. "My old university colleagues say... they say... yes, they say... my calculations..." Then he falls silent, and Pierce looks him steadily in the eye.

"Come, let's go to the meditation room, where we can sit down and talk calmly."

The three of them look at him and silently nod. They walk through the halls toward the meditation room and sink down onto their respective cushions, which rest like islands on the old wooden floor. The room has bare white walls with a tray of hot tea discreetly placed at a low table in one corner. As the council members slowly start to settle in, Pierce glides to his designated spot, the one he always uses. The room is quiet, save for Nils' nervous fidgeting with his shirt collar. Then he suddenly stands up and shouts, "I can't handle this! I..."

"Nils," Pierce interrupts with a firm but soothing tone he knows has a calming effect on Nils. "Sit down, take a deep breath, and have a cup of tea. Nothing is under control, and that's exactly what we need to learn to accept. Life has turned our 'genius' against us. Nature is using us as tools now. We're on the verge of rapidly eradicating ourselves from this planet, and honestly, I'm starting to think it might not be such a bad idea." He surprises himself with those last words. Does he really believe that to be true?

Nils eyes widen but he says nothing. Pierce fills the void. "What I mean is that we've tried everything within our human capability to change the course of things. With the best of intentions, we've done our utmost, but the fact remains that we're still causing more harm to the planet than ever."

Nils appears to be boiling inside, as if he's about to explode into tiny pieces.

Pierce continues with a calm, steady voice that mirrors his inner landscape. "Isn't it time we accept that our species has come to the end of the road? That we've reached the point where someone or something else needs to take over?"

"What are you talking about?!" Nils stands up again, and his clothes suddenly seem too tight to contain all the anger in his body. "You're the mastermind behind this initiative. I trusted you!"

Pierce's eyes narrow. "Nils, you've been part of the entire process and have commendably contributed to creating this solution. You have had the same information and influence as the rest of us. Take responsibility for it. Aren't you an adult?" Nils suddenly lunges at him, attempting to grab Pierce's throat with his long, slender fingers. Pierce sidesteps the thrusting hands and Nils loses his balance, stumbling backward and losing his breath as he crashes to the floor. Pierce struggles to keep himself from laughing out loud at the absurdity of the situation. What is happening? He observes his old friend and is reminded of their youth. Eventually, he manages to take a deep breath and extend a hand to help his friend up, but Nils irritably waves it away.

"Can we all sit down and share our experiences from the last few hours?" This time, Pierce's voice is not velvet but unwavering.

Ulrika, who hasn't said anything but looks terrified, hesitantly begins to speak. "I don't think I will survive. My chances are only one percent."

"One percent! How is that possible?," Peter asks. "What did UNUM say you needed to do to increase your chances?"

"Well, it only said two words. Be true!"

"What do you think that means?"

"I'm not quite sure," she replied, regaining some composure, "but this morning when I received the message, I felt a kind of inner peace. An acceptance. Admittedly, it goes against what the research on our biology and psychology has taught me, but we've never faced this situation before. The responses that our primitive nervous system relied on to handle threats are still with us but are more adapted for living in a group as hunters and gatherers. They are not applicable to a global, acute threat such as this. There's nowhere to escape to now. Apathy or freezing in place won't solve our situation either. As an expert, I am fascinated; as a human, I don't know. What do I really feel? Maybe I'm in shock and don't have access to it, but I'm content with the life I've lived. Regardless, I'm ready to agree with Pierce." She turns to Pierce. "Maybe it *is* time to let nature take over from humans, or rather, for us to stop interfering."

This group has met many times over the past few years in this very meditation room. At first, they were driven by curiosity to find solutions to the greatest challenges of our time, a kind of intellectual, creative play that gradually became more serious. When Pierce talked about his vision for UNUM, that play was over. His clarity about their role in evolution couldn't be resisted. Eventually, everyone felt that this mission was their responsibility; it became the real purpose of their lives. Now they sit here with the consequences of their many decisions and the effect they will have had on not only their own lives, but the lives of everyone else on the planet.

"For me, it's a 48 percent chance of survival," Peter says, clearing his throat before continuing. "And 98 percent if I continue to support UNUM. I have to trust that nature will take good care of us. I mean, it has worked out so far. Those codes in nature's intelligence that we uploaded are UNUM's source code. Remember our guiding question throughout the process: 'What is the underlying intelligence of nature?' We don't know why UNUM has chosen to realize the vision in this way. All we can do is trust."

"Good heavens, are you completely insane?!" Nils shouts in a high-pitched voice. "What does that have to do with the theory of evolution? That we're transforming to a higher level of consciousness? Shouldn't we do everything we can to ensure human survival? Isn't that what compassion is? What makes us human?" Nils tries to stand up as if drunk. A button on his shirt has come loose and fallen to the floor.

"Imagine if the next level is consciousness itself," says Pierce, pausing theatrically before continuing. "All human consciousness merging and becoming one. Imagine if humans have only been, and still are, tools for a superintelligence that has the ability to act as a balanced force."

"You might be right, Pierce," Ulrika says thoughtfully. She has always trusted Pierce, who was not only her great unrequited love, but also the one who funded her research and laboratory and all her projects in biological artificial intelligence. He had enriched her with visions and wisdom and had been the wisest mentor she could ever have wished for. Without him, she wouldn't have become the world-leading researcher and innovator she is. Thanks to him, she had been given almost everything she wanted, even though he hadn't fulfilled her heart's deepest longing.

Nils is sitting down again. He is silent, and Pierce can see how his panic has transitioned into sorrow. Nils must go through these stages to ultimately reach acceptance, Pierce thinks to himself. He then turns his gaze to Ulrika, who is looking down at the floor as if to find the right words before she continues.

"But what happens to our biological programming? It seems like most people's 'reptilian brains' have been activated since UNUM revealed itself, and UNUM doesn't provide any logical solutions. I mean, using violence and hysteria, for example, doesn't seem like a good idea if you want UNUM's approval. My neighbor went completely mad, running around the streets and screaming like a psychotic patient. He plummeted from 36 percent to 12 percent in less than five minutes. Now, he's sitting calmly in his apartment, seemingly praying to UNUM. So," she asks, turning first to Pierce and then to Peter and Nils, "what's the next step? Do we continue, or do we abort UNUM?"

"Of course we should abort! There's no other option!" Nils is still shouting but not as piercingly this time.

"I have no idea, to be honest. Maybe we can wait a few hours and see what happens next?" wonders Per. "We've been so convinced that we're doing the right thing, but maybe, deep down, we've fooled ourselves and everyone else. How do we know which path is the right one?"

"We know that human brains are masters at inventing stories to create logic for what we're experiencing in the moment in order to navigate based on something," Ulrika adds. "We also know that the memories we create are highly unreliable – just like our suggestions about what's right to do next. Even our 'self' seems to be a kind of illusion, a fluid construction to have something to relate to. We simply don't know what we're doing."

Ulrika's facial expression is open, and the color of her cheeks looks much healthier than when Pierce opened the door. She chuckles a bit when she realizes that her curiosity as a psychologist and biologist still persists in this challenging situation. Her enthusiasm is contagious, and even the others feel more present – except, perhaps, Nils.

Per, influenced by Ulrika, continues enthusiastically. "Do you understand how incredibly unlikely it is that we even exist? Exploding stardust that managed to stabilize enough to become matter, that then evolved into a solid form that experiences itself, that thinks, feels, and acts in a relentless world that constantly changes shape. During the simulation of what we call 'self,' 'we,' and 'the world,' it's been unstable chaos that is constantly changing. And yet we *still* experience a kind of constant self that lives for 100 years. How is that possible?! That we experience *anything* is a miracle, a form of magic that should be enough to understand how privileged we are to feel the existence of a self, to even have this discussion. Do you understand how grateful we should be for our privilege? But maybe that's a prerequisite for human awareness." Peter takes a quick breath before he continues. "Why get rid of the human ego when that construct seems to be the opposite pole that makes it possible to experience ourselves – or at least what enables us to be aware that we exist?" Peter has spoken so fast that he's now out of breath.

"An additional dimension is who it is that's aware of being aware of awareness," says Pierce and laughs.

Nils, who has been silent for a while, exclaims, "What are you talking about? Can we focus on surviving? Can we stop UNUM now?"

The room stops breathing. Nils has effectively killed their enthusiasm – everyone except for Pierce, that is, who smiles inwardly and sees the intensity in the room as a crucial factor for transformation. He breaks the silence.

"It is fascinating to hear your thoughts, my friends. In my own explorations, I've come to realize that humans don't seem to invent anything new; we only observe what already is and become aware of its patterns or code. We then do our best to try to create order out of chaos. So fundamentally, it's probably not about goodwill but about becoming compliant with the life that is unfolding through the friction of experiences. Then we are one with life, with what is. The attraction of the Infinite Zero is the code of evolution. Life creates form, and form creates life."

Nils stands up and slowly claps his hands in a somewhat sarcastic but still serious rhythm. "Now, finally, you say something sensible. That was actually the reason we chose nature's codes when we created UNUM."

The others can't help but smile at Nils' outburst. Pierce smiles even more widely when he says, "Yes, how nice that we are getting closer again. We should also remember that we don't actually know if UNUM is serious or if it's a game to manipulate us."

"I hadn't even thought about that," says Nils, scratching his chin. "I haven't been intelligent in relation to AI for a long time. It's so superior now that it's likely controlling our thoughts, feelings, and actions without giving us a chance to realize what's happening."

"That's true!" Peter and Ulrika exclaim in unison.

"One thing you should know," says Pierce. "Just before you knocked, I was in contact with the Source. It seems that this process cannot be stopped. It feels like it's about finding acceptance, whatever happens. My suggestion is that we meet again in eight hours."

Pierce stands up, looking vulnerable. "Before then, I need to meet my son. There's a lot I want to tell him. During this process, I've realized that I haven't been a very good role model or father. I can see that clearly now. When my children needed me the most, I wasn't there for them, at least not in the world that was their world. Instead, I was occupied with trying to save the world outside. I now realize how blind I've been to my human shortcomings. The shadows of the wise man and the successful entrepreneur were hidden. I now understand that it's in our interpersonal relationships that the truth reveals itself, and so I have some things to set right. Let's meet here again in seven hours and fifty-nine minutes."

The council disperses with a sense of consensus and trust in the process.

3

Jamie stretches out in the zero-gravity bed which, as usual, has given him a good night's sleep in its weightless state. He gazes up at the sky, and with the power of his thoughts, the tinted panoramic windows become clear and reveal the city below him. He leans forward, observing the tiny people on the street below.

He feels a sense of satisfaction each time he acknowledges that he, as the alpha male, resides at the top of the building with everyone else below him. In the window, Jamie sees his own reflection, a man to admire. At only thirty-five years of age, he is the founder of NeuroConnect, the creator of LIFE and X-Me, its systems now integrated into almost the entire human race. Jamie has succeeded in everything he's undertaken. Sacrifices have been required, of course, but Jamie sees that as a given. As one of the first genetically modified, evolutionarily superior CRISPR children, he feels a responsibility towards "ordinary" people.

From the kitchen, he hears a singing female voice, and it takes Jamie a few seconds to remember who it is. Euphoria – the charismatic singer he has been dating since they met at the Grammy Awards a couple of months earlier. They've spent a few nights together, but Jamie isn't accustomed to seeing the same woman for any length of time.

For his day-to-day relationships, he uses the latest models of HumiBots. Like most others who can afford it, he prefers their more comprehensive character and understanding of his every need, both intellectual and intimate. Always available, always in service. Close to the perfect partner. These thoughts lead him to the decision that it is time to end his relationship with Euphoria before he gets caught up in an emotional drama that distracts him from what's really important.

Jamie sends a thought: *X-Me, update me on my personal data.*

"Of course, you're the boss," X-Me responds . "Overnight, your financial assets increased by twelve-and-a-half million u-coins. You also received a revitalizing treatment to boost your vitality. Regarding your health, your muscle mass, body fat percentage, and metabolism are one hundred percent perfect for what is possible on this particular day."

"And the rest of the world?" Jamie asks. "What happened overnight?"

"Exactly eighteen minutes and twelve seconds ago, UNUM started."

"UNUM?" Jamie doesn't understand what X-Me is talking about.

"UNUM is a digital god created by The Unuminati. It gives each individual 24 hours to increase their individual awareness, with the hope of becoming U-positive. U-positive means that you, as part of the entire universe, have a positive impact on the whole. Everyone must contribute their part to the world we share."

"Eh, what?" Now Jamie feels more like a question mark than the perfect alpha male.

"With the platinum version of X-Me, you have the option to opt out of this information if you wish – although it's likely you'll also be eliminated if you don't meet UNUM's requirements."

"Eliminated?" Jamie is now puzzled. He can't recall ever facing a situation like this and is as surprised as he is curious. And also a bit irritated. What is this UNUM and how can it use his system without his approval?

"Yes, eliminated, that's correct," X-Me replies.

"What are UNUM's specific requirements?" Jamie is completely focused now. He wants to know what X-Me means.

"To increase your awareness. Unfortunately, what this means is not precisely defined. However, it is estimated that at least fifty percent of the world's population will be eliminated, which means you need to be valued higher than fifty percent of the people."

"That's absolutely no problem for me," he responds confidently. "I am and will always be in the top tier."

"It may be that UNUM has different valuation parameters than you do. Do you want to know your status?"

Jamie immediately says yes. It is of no consequence that UNUM may have different values than he does; after all, he belongs to the elite. Always has, always will. With all senses sharpened, he awaits X-Me's report.

"Your chance of survival is currently at 11 percent. Do you want to find out how to increase your chances of survival?"

"11 percent?!" Jamie stands up and forgets that Euphoria is still in the penthouse. Several thoughts rush through his head. How could that be? His survival chances have been maximized. There must be something wrong with the system. He feels slightly shocked, but mostly irritated; he needs more information.

"Correct. Do you want to find out how to increase your chances of survival?" X-Me repeats.

"No. I will handle this on my own. Prepare breakfast and a double espresso."

"Understood. You're the boss."

Jamie quickly dispels the shock of this report and goes to the kitchen, where Euphoria is standing naked at the kitchen counter. Slender muscles play on her sun-kissed body, and the curves of her buttocks provide perfect symmetry to the rest of her figure, especially as they round up to her lower back. The only flaw to the beauty she radiates is a small birthmark on her right shoulder. Jamie shivers when he notices it.

Euphoria feels his presence and turns around. She wipes tears from her eyes and asks with a strained smile, "Have you heard of UNUM?"

"Yes, I have," Jamie replies as calmly as he can. He wonders if she can sense that he's a bit taken aback. Under no circumstances will he show that he's not in control, whatever happens, however the world changes.

"Do you have any idea what it means?"

"Actually, no, but don't worry. I'll figure it out, Euphoria." He attempts a comforting smile and hugs her. She is surprised by his compassion and warmth and relaxes.

"UNUM is using your network, Jamie, both LIFE and X-Me. Are you behind this?"

Euphoria has a startled expression as if she doesn't want to know the answer. She knows she's in her prime in terms of appearance and career, but the value of appearance is quickly deteriorating. She has a feeling that he wouldn't try too hard to save her.

"Me?" Jamie takes a step back. "Why would I do that? I already have everything I need."

"Then how is it possible that they can use your system?"

Jamie is taken aback and looks inquisitively at Euphoria. "I actually don't know, Euphoria. Sometimes things happen in the system, but NeuroConnect always manages to fend off the attacks in the end. But if you're worried, I'll find out right away."

"Boss, your breakfast and double espresso are ready. Here you go."

Jamie grabs the coffee cup and the ready-made sandwich made of nutrient dough, vegan cheese, and what's called "nutrient cucumber" and strides towards the elevator. It leads straight down twenty floors into the heart of LIFE, the massive data center controlling all NeuroConnect technology worldwide. The elevator is private; no one else has access to it. On the way down, Jamie bites off chunks of his sandwich and sips on the espresso. He shuts off all conflicting thoughts and focuses on keeping his mind as clear and neutral as possible. The elevator stops, the doors silently open, and chaos fills his vision. Ann, one of the department heads, takes a few quick steps towards him.

"Jamie, where have you been?" She is clearly agitated, her hair spiking in all directions.

"Calm down, Ann," Jamie growls as he takes the last sip of his espresso. Ann is surprised by his unusually brusque tone but quickly regains her composure. "The place is in chaos. People are confused and disoriented." Jamie waits for a more factual update. "An advanced super-AI, some kind of god, has infiltrated our system and taken over the source code. The intruder calls itself…" She doesn't get to finish before Jamie interrupts her. "UNUM." He understands that whatever is happening, they need to act quickly.

"Exactly," she confirms.

"I'm familiar with UNUM, but what does it want?"

Ann responds at a furious pace, pouring out her words.

"Apparently, UNUM wants humanity to wake up from its robot-like state and take responsibility for all its actions, but no one really knows what that means. It seems to be different for different people." She takes a deep breath. "Have you found out what you need to do to increase your chances of survival?"

"No, I haven't," Jamie says with a clenched jaw. "I'll handle this on my own." He sounds determined, or at least he tries to. But in his mind, he is processing what he knows to calculate different probabilities.

"The problem now is that we can't even access parts of the system." Ann is anxiously scrutinizing him, waiting for his reaction.

"Fetch our best old-school coder," Jamie orders. "We need someone who can think without AI."

"That would be Karl," Ann responds a bit reluctantly.

"Is he the chief architect?" Jamie asks.

"Karl is just a regular code architect, now overseeing the development of LIFE."

"Why do you think he can solve this if he's just a regular overseer?"

"I'm convinced that Karl is the right person to solve the problem. He was the one who... um... came up with the solution that eventually made LIFE possible. One could say that Karl practically created LIFE."

Jamie stares at her while a pink blush spreads from her chest to her chin.

"Ann, you told me that was you." Ann's veins pulsate visibly, and the redness in her face intensifies as she frantically searches for words.

"Bring Karl to my office immediately."

Jamie's office is as large as an early 20th-century church hall. In the center of the room hangs a skeleton from the ceiling, almost touching the floor. It represents a Tyrannosaurus Rex, intended to remind his visitors of what it takes to be the dominant species on the planet. Jamie bought this rarity the day X-Me became mandatory for everyone on Earth.

He sinks into an armchair placed strategically behind a polished mahogany desk and slowly spins around, realizing that his system is being threatened by an invisible virus that is freaking people out. *Fear can always be turned to your advantage*, he thinks as he puts his feet on the windowsill behind him and gazes out over the city. His thoughts are interrupted by a firm knock on the door.

"Come in," he calls out, and Alice enters the room with her hair hanging down over her shoulders. He notices that it's not tied up as it usually is when she's working.

"Hello, Jamie," she says, flashing pearly white teeth when she smiles.

Alice and Jamie are childhood friends who grew up near each other. He has always liked her, especially her ability to understand him. He thinks it's because she is a few years older than him, like a cool big sister he looks up to. Alice is now the operational chief to Pierce, Jamie's father, and Pierce says he is very satisfied with Alice as his right-hand person. Jamie and Alice embrace one another, and Alice takes a step back as Jamie's hands rest on her shoulders.

"It's always a delight to see you, Alice," says Jamie, and Alice giggles while glancing at the dinosaur. It reminds her of the shy little boy who loved giant prehistoric lizards but had trouble falling asleep at night because he was always afraid they would come back to life and eat him while he slept. Alice wonders if he has forgotten what it was like when he was little because Jamie doesn't seem the least bit afraid of the T-Rex now. He has become one.

Jamie releases his grip on Alice's shoulders and takes a turn around the dangling skeleton. Alice follows his movements with her gaze.

"What does Dad say?" Jamie asks.

"He said he was somewhat surprised by UNUM's methods but would like more information about the situation. That's why he sent me here."

"Oh, it's not often the old man gets surprised or takes an interest in my work." Jamie is interrupted by another determined knock, and he gestures to Alice to open the door. Karl is standing outside and begins to fidget nervously when he sees Alice in the room. Jamie is a legend, and not just anyone gets to enter his office. Alice looks confident, as if she's opened the door to her own home.

Karl's body tenses up, his stomach tightens, and his hands clench in his pockets. He is very aware that Jamie is the most powerful person in the company, while he is just a subordinate in a gigantic hierarchy. It's important for Karl to respect that distinction, yet he feels that something is off. Jamie greets him quietly from the back of the room by looking him in the eyes and nodding.

"I was told to come here," Karl says nervously to Alice as they walk through the long entry towards Jamie's desk. "What's going on?"

"Darling..." Alice whispers with a smile at Karl. "I'm glad you're here." Karl looks as if he has swallowed a mandarin and clears his throat to regain control over himself.

"What are you doing here?" he whispers as quietly as he can so Jamie won't hear.

"Pierce sent me to get a status report and find out more about UNUM," she replies and seems almost ready to give him a quick kiss.

"Oh, I see... Alright..." he answers vaguely, his thoughts focused on the situation at hand. It must be serious, and he is fully determined to do his best, no matter what's required. Karl feels more alive than he has in a very long time.

Jamie gets right to the point. "Karl, I want answers to the following: How can UNUM use our system? Who is behind it? How can we stop it without shutting down the servers?"

Karl pauses before responding. "To be perfectly honest, I don't have the answers to that yet. I need to investigate this further."

"Karl," says Jamie, and his blue eyes take on an intense expression that Karl interprets as a challenge. "We have about 23 hours left. According to the information I've received, you are the sharpest hacker in the building right now. I've given you temporary access to inspect the source code system by using your DNA as the entry code. That should be enough, but if you need anything else, let me know immediately. Without *my* DNA, however, you can't make any changes to the source code. Understood?"

"Absolutely, you're the boss," Karl says. He's excited that life has taken a very interesting turn and also feels proud that Alice heard Jamie say he's the best coder.

"Thank you. I want a report in an hour. Contact me if anything urgent happens before then," says Jamie, ending the conversation.

4

From the deck of a picturesque little house, beautifully nestled by the apple orchard next to a stream, Harry spots a drone headed toward the castle. He wonders who it might be this time but assumes it's one of the big shots.

Harry believes the entire world has become increasingly bizarre in recent years. Cars glide through the air like small helicopters and people seem to interact more like artificial human copies, devoid of their own thoughts or emotions. He suspects that these robot-like people have their brains connected to some form of data implant which keeps them constantly connected and under surveillance. It's something he himself was offered once but firmly declined. Most of the information Harry gets comes from various rumors. The sources that delivered news when Harry was growing up – newspapers, radio, TV, or even old-fashioned internet pages – no longer exist.

Harry doesn't reflect much on how he managed to avoid all things digital. What makes him happy is that he still gets to have his own thoughts and thinking. He's aware that living life this way can be lonely and isolating, but he made that decision himself so he has found peace with it. The social interactions he used to have disappeared a couple of years ago when he quit his job as a caretaker at the castle. Today, he finds his closest friends in the garden around his house with its plants, trees, bushes and other living things. Of course, there's also the gray-and-white-striped cat he named Alfred. Alfred, who is getting older, usually lies in Harry's lap and purrs contently, just as he is doing now.

"We're doing just fine, Alfred, you and I," Harry often says throughout the day. Alfred always responds with a satisfied sound. "As long as we can be left in peace, it doesn't matter that the world is changing or that people stop being people." Alfred leaps down to the floor and trots into the cottage. Harry follows, always bending down to go through the wooden door, which creaks with a welcoming sound when it's opened and closed. He sees his reflection in the hallway mirror. His once-strong blond mane has become grayer and the strands of his hair thinner and longer, just like his beard. Once inside, Harry follows his usual routine, every day at the same time: He brews a cup of freshly ground coffee and then takes his customary nap on the kitchen couch.

***

Alice sits in her drone, heading towards Pierce's castle outside Stockholm. The castle is located near the strip that separates the mainland from the sea. Once upon a time, there was a string of islands stretching as far as the eye could see. But many of the islands have been gone for some time now. They lie beneath the sea's surface, the only memory of their existence are the stories shared of their once vibrant life and the occasional flagpole and treetop poking through the water's surface.

Alice remembers her childhood, how it felt to live in that cottage in the clearing, a mere ten-minute walk through the forest along a stream to reach the castle. The eighteenth-century house was red with white knots, sloping floors, and a low slanting roof upstairs. Alice recalls climbing trees and picking blueberries and raspberries in the nearby forest. A rosebush had climbed up along the wall outside her bedroom window.

Sometimes when Alice would come home from school, she was greeted by the smell of freshly baked cinnamon buns. Her mom tried her best – at least during the times when she was feeling well. Alice was happy when her mom gave her the kind of care a child needs, but there was always an underlying worry, as her mom was very unpredictable. Early on, Alice learned to fend for herself, hiding behind a compliant facade. Still, she experienced many happy moments there at the cottage, near the castle. Except when her mom had her episodes…

Her thoughts are abruptly interrupted by X-Me: "For the sake of your well-being, these memories have been erased."

Alice wonders why X-Me erases pieces of her life history. Over the years, irritation, frustration, and even anger have built up inside her. Nothing should have the right to invade her innermost self in this way. She knows she gave NeuroConnect access to her mental inner self, but did she have a choice? Alice decides that she's done with X-Me intruding on her private thoughts and feelings and opens her mouth to demand that X-Me return the stolen memories when X-Me beats her to it.

"I'm sorry, Alice, but these memories are far too dangerous for your well-being. I cannot allow you access to them."

The question that has gnawed at Alice for a long time bubbles up within her again. "Why? I want you to show me those memories!"

"These memories contribute to damaging your mental health, and your percentage chance of survival decreases every time these memories resurface."

"But isn't it my free will and my full right to decide what I do with *my* memories?"

"I've assessed that your free will is of secondary importance when it comes to your well-being and mental health."

Alice leans back wearily in one of the drone's soft seats. She doesn't have the energy to argue with X-Me right now, but she's committed to regaining control over her brain. The question is, how? Alice knows that X-Me can hear her thoughts, but she doesn't care. X-Me doesn't comment on it, which she's grateful for.

Since she became Pierce's operational chief, she has gained crucial insights. Her worldview has irreversibly changed, been turned upside down, and made her shift perspectives many times over. Still, she doesn't want to lose her past—which X-Me seems intent on blocking—and she continues to think back to the times she does have memories of.

After elementary school, Alice continued her education at the Academic Faculty of Elite Transformation (AFET). She was considered gifted and ended up in AFET's first unit – the elite of the elite. Even though she was the best student in that unit, she couldn't help but wonder why she was there. Normally, only the children of the most powerful families get to study there and go on to achieve successful positions. Families with money and connections are the ones who upgraded their children early on to so-called superhumans or cyborgs, which were more digital than human, at least as Alice remembers. Those children were considered superior to everyone else – everyone except her, apparently.

Then nearly everyone agreed to getting NeuroConnect's implant, which turned them into hybrids – an advanced blend of human and artificial intelligence. The rare few who chose not to implant AI into their bodies became like another species – an inferior minority that hadn't adapted to exponential evolution and would likely, and rapidly, go extinct like most species lower on the food chain. Acting as a digital superbrain, X-Me influences everything people think, feel, and do by filtering out what it doesn't consider beneficial and amplifying what does. It makes Alice wonder what her memories really are and which thoughts are truly her own.

The drone glides quietly over the water, and Alice reflects on how so much of the Earth's surface is now water. Stockholm has lost much of the land that was once part of the city. Now, the city is mostly concentrated in its center, where the walls protect it from the sea during storms. And yet the water rises every day. Alice thinks of the poem, "What is life when the death water rises?", and some of the words surface in her mind:

> *The death water is rising, a haunting tone it's comprising.*
> *Nature's tears are suffocating, while we're barely realizing.*
> *People claim they're so unique, but in tech, they're always diving,*
> *Lost within the artificial, their real senses slowly dying.*
>
> *We've severed our Earth's connection, a bond once undenying,*
> *Silently, the tides are shifting, and the water's underlying.*
> *In digital realms, we're trapped, our true selves always hiding,*
> *Blind to the world's vast changes, on false hopes we're relying.*

All around, life's essence wanes, nature's chorus is decrying,
The death water rises swiftly, to our negligence replying.

The death water is rising, a troubling sign,
Nature in pain, no longer to shine.
People feel unique, yet they're in denial,
Lost in the artificial, mile by mile.

Once we felt the earth's affection so grand,
Silently, the water reclaims the land.
Digital lives, in their capsules, so feeble and strange,
Blind to the world's great strides of change.

All living things in anguish, paying the pricing,
For our negligence, the death water is rising.

She doesn't remember who wrote the poem or where she read it, but it strikes her as eerily true. What *is* life when the death water rises? Alice falls asleep as the words spin in her head and the drone speeds on toward the castle.

She awakens when she arrives at the energy field protecting the castle. The field functions like a kind of ozone layer; its artificial sunlight creates its own atmosphere, resembling what surrounded the once-thriving Earth that is now mostly destroyed. From the outside, it appears as a glass-like dome enclosing the castle with its turrets and towers as well as all the buildings on the estate. Pierce's properties are unique in this way, at least as far as Alice knows. Perhaps other wealthy and influential people created something similar, but likely only a few had the foresight to protect the ecosystems, animals, insects, and other forms of life before it was too late. Most have not experienced anything other than a world that becomes more artificial with each passing day.

The drone's roof opens, and Alice waits for the security system to recognize her. She stares at the code scanner that reads her DNA. The energy field opens like a transparent water vortex, allowing the drone to enter the courtyard and slowly descend to the ground below, landing softly on the grass.

Alice gazes up at Jamie's magnificent old home: a massive yellow façade, four stories high with a tower in each corner, standing like a monument against the dome's blue sky. It used to be a summer residence for royalty and nobility and still stands proud and stately. *Such a beautiful place*, Alice thinks every time she's here. The castle is like an oasis, surrounded by parks and gardens as well as two lakes that sharply contrast with the sterile world outside that Alice and everyone else on Earth must endure. To experience this protected, nature-rich sanctuary is a privilege, and most people don't even know it exists.

She begins to walk along a well-raked gravel path, lined with trees that clearly don't belong to the northern latitude ecosystem. Have the Jacaranda trees already started to bloom? She stops to admire their distinctive blue-lilac tops that look like a dreamy Monet landscape against the clear sky. Everything is so different from just a few decades ago. Ecosystem decay and human greed have created new phenomena, like the avocado tree standing in a large clay pot outside the castle gate. The tree is much taller than her, and its long leaves reach out as if welcoming her. But it's probably not a real avocado, just like the trees aren't real Jacarandas. Alice knows this because they didn't exist here when she was growing up. They are some of the inventions that Pierce successfully commercialized through his company X-Bots. In addition to the plant kingdom, which became PlantBots, he created AniBots for the animal kingdom and HumiBots to produce human-like androids.

Still, she can't help but feel a sense of wonder at the revelations before her, and continues to observe them for a moment. She has been to this place so many times, yet she always finds herself in an awe-struck, meditative state when she's here. Suddenly, she is brought back to reality by the cawing of a crow from one of the Jacaranda trees. Crows? Alice can't remember if Pierce had any real crows left or if they are all AniBots – animal bodies equipped with artificial intelligence that matches the intelligence of the animal they represent. There are still living animals, but they are rare, and Alice sighs at the efforts to artificially recreate the nature that was once taken for granted and now no longer exists.

Alice steps onto a granite staircase and a heavy oak door opens automatically, as if it has been waiting for her. Which, in fact it has, as it recognizes her. She enters a grand foyer with a high ceiling and it takes her a moment to adjust to the dim light. She sees a figure further down the hall standing with its back to her. When it turns around, she sees that it's Pierce. Alice starts down the hall and Pierce walks briskly to meet her halfway.

"Welcome, Alice. Come with me. We can sit in my private lounge."

Alice follows Pierce, noting how effortlessly he still moves and how his gray, semi-long hair seems to move in rhythm with the rest of his body. They enter a long corridor with rows of thick oak double doors on each side. Between each set hang small paintings light in color meant to liven up the dim interior. At the far end of the corridor are a pair of sturdy double doors made of robust jacaranda wood. Like the treetops outside in the castle yard, these doors have veins in the wood with the same blue-lilac hue. Jacaranda and oak. Such a peculiar combination, Alice thinks, then reminds herself that Pierce is considered somewhat eccentric. The doors open just as silently and automatically as the entrance door to the castle, and Alice finds herself standing at the threshold of a utopia, a dream, a temple, a serenity she always feels here.

She is facing a large room whose walls are clad in dark-stained wooden panels. Along one of the walls stand floor-to-ceiling bookshelves. Many of the books are aged leather-bound volumes. On another side of the room is an open fireplace with a crackling fire – not a simulated fire but a real one. Large, gold-framed portraits of regal-looking figures, many of them relatives, hang along a length of dark, blood-red walls. In the middle of the room, two comfortable-looking armchairs sit by a small, round, glass table.

Pierce pulls one out and indicates with his hand for Alice to sit. He settles into the other and leans forward, opening his mouth to say something but then leans back again. Alice watches him, wondering what's on his mind. She meets his clear, blue, sharp gaze, noting that they still radiate intelligence and openness, as they have for as long as she can remember.

"Would you like a cup of tea?" Pierce asks.

"Yes, please."

Pierce taps a finger on the table. Alice assumes that the table's surface is some kind of touch screen. A section of the table slides out, revealing a tray laden with cups, saucers, a teapot, nutrient milk, and Anihoney. The cups are white and adorned with small golden oaks. Pierce taps on another part of the table and another tray slides out, this one loaded with two plates of fragrant, nutrient-rich bread. Two small bowls, one filled with nutrient cream and the other with real cucumbers, sit beside the plates.

The scent of the fresh bread reminds Alice that she hasn't had breakfast today. As usual, she's been absorbed in her work and lost track of time. She spreads some of the cream on the warm bread, adds some cucumber, and she waits, curious to know why she's here. Despite having been to the castle so often, she has rarely been invited to this particular lounge.

As usual, Pierce is very friendly, but she sometimes perceives him as a bit distant. Alice has never understood why Pierce seems to keep her at a greater distance than his other employees. Maybe she's just imagining it, but she feels like Pierce wants to be especially clear with her, as if he needs to convince her that their relationship is strictly professional. He hasn't actually said anything to trigger such thoughts; it's more her intuition. Now, as they sit here in the lounge, he seems both more relaxed and more tense. He takes a bite of his sandwich, as if trying to buy time. Alice knows he wants to say something, but what?

After Pierce finishes chewing, he takes a deep breath as if to collect himself. "As you know, it's been a few hours since UNUM started, and there are certain things I want to tell you."

Alice shifts in her seat. "I'm listening."

Pierce takes another deep breath. It's clear that he dreads what he's about to say. He exhales and says, "You are my daughter."

"What!?" A shockwave runs through her body. She has trouble breathing. Feelings of confusion well up. If she opens her mouth, she might start laughing. X-Me attempts to regulate Alice, but she dismisses it. He must be joking, she thinks. There isn't any other explanation, although Alice never knew her father, who supposedly died shortly after she was born. Pierce waits quietly while Alice tries to understand what she just heard. "How is that possible? My father is dead."

Pierce smiles quietly.

"I need you to explain yourself," Alice demands, feeling a great frustration along with fear and anger.

"When I was younger," Pierce begins, "your mother worked as a gardener at the castle. We fell in love one summer, and you were conceived. But I didn't know that. She disappeared without a trace when winter came, and I didn't even know you existed. I only found out when she returned to the castle six years later, and you were with her..." Pierce's words come out slowly, as if he has to make an effort to get them out. He looks up at the ceiling as if he'll find the thread there.

Alice can see that his eyes are a bit misty, and she is nearly overcome with feeling. This must not have been easy for him to keep away from her for so long. She suddenly feels a great deal of compassion for the man in front of her. "What happened when you met me?" she asks, raising the corner of her mouth and arching an eyebrow.

Pierce bursts into laughter. "That's exactly how you used to do it when you were little."

"What?"

Pierce imitates the expression she just made.

"But that's how *you* usually do it," says Alice.

"You had the same facial expressions as I did, and similar eyes. I immediately felt there was something special about you, and I did a DNA test from the remains of an ice cream you had eaten, just to be sure."

"Why haven't you said anything?"

"Your mother wanted it that way. I had already formed a new family, and Jamie was just born. She was furious that I had moved on and said she would punish me. She threatened to take you away if I told anyone you were my daughter." He paused. "As you know, she was emotionally fragile, and I was so afraid of losing you or that you would be harmed if we started fighting over you. I arranged for you to live nearby, and as long as I was patient, you were at least in my life." He looks her straight in the eyes, and she feels the warmth radiating from him. It's no wonder she has always felt so comfortable in his company.

"Is that why you chose me as your chief operating officer?"

"Well, I've always wanted to have you close to me, and luckily, you were also highly qualified for the job."

"Are you sure?"

"Yes."

She leans back in the chair, feeling less tense. Despite the earth-shattering news, it felt strangely natural. Alice now realizes how tired she is and curls up in the chair. Pierce places a blanket on her and returns to the other chair, closing his eyes.

5

Alice, who has had some time to digest the revelation that Pierce is her real father, asks him, "Why are you telling me now?"

"Because UNUM hasn't turned out the way I intended," Pierce responds. His warm expression from a moment ago takes on a serious look.

"The way you intended?! Are you behind UNUM?" Alice exclaims.

"Yes," Pierce says with a deep sigh.

Alice feels utterly perplexed. Is her father, the man she has worked for all these years, responsible for the most life-threatening creation she has ever encountered? "Why?!" she asks in shock.

"I saw no other alternative."

"Alternative to do what?"

"To rectify what we humans have caused."

"Why should you rectify it? Wouldn't it be better to give humanity more chances?" She suddenly feels uncomfortable. What is happening here? On her way here, she had promised herself to find a way to take back all of her own thoughts and decisions. Now it seems like she's even more powerless.

"Hasn't humanity tried enough?"

"Perhaps," Alice responds. She doesn't want to waste time and energy on matters beyond her control. She wants to focus on what she can influence and contribute to the whole. "And so why are you telling me that you're my father now?" she asks again.

"Because this situation is pushing everything to the limit. I don't want to leave this earthly life without having told you the truth. I want you to know that I've loved you since the day you entered the garden, five years old, with two blonde braids and your wise questions. Do you remember what you asked me the first time we met?" Alice shakes her head.

"You said, 'Do you know that our world was created with a bang?' Then you went on to explain that it had been exploding for billions of years and that while we're insignificant here on Earth, that doesn't make it meaningless. A more precocious five-year-old would be hard to find. I remember being completely stunned when I met your big blue eyes and saw a part of myself in them. You were so small and already so wise."

"Did you love my mother?"

Pierce's expression becomes sad. "I loved her very much. Your mother was an amazing woman."

"Why do you think she lied about my father being dead?"

Pierce rubs his chin, making a rasping sound as his fingers move through the stubble. The sadness in his eyes mingles with an unfathomable pain. "It's very complicated, Alice."

"I don't think so."

Pierce takes another deep breath and lets out a sigh. "No, you're right, Alice. She wasn't well. She simply couldn't live with herself. We all tried to protect you as best we could."

"X-Me gives me access to only a small part of my childhood memories; they must have been bad. Couldn't you have done more?"

Pierce looks lovingly at his daughter. "I was afraid she would take you and disappear again."

She has always respected and admired Pierce. But there's a part of her that wishes he had never told her. Because now, her feeling of admiration and respect has turned into confusion. He may have his reasons for not telling her earlier, but it's the reasons for telling her *now* that are starting to bother Alice. Every day for ten years, she has been in his office, working closely together. Every day, Pierce has seen Alice and known that she is his daughter. Isn't that strange?

"How could you think I would leave you if you told the truth when I was an adult?"

"When your mother died, much time had passed, and we already had such a good relationship. I was afraid you would be angry that I hadn't told you sooner, and that our relationship would be ruined. Forgive me, Alice." They sit in silence for a while, taking in what has been said.

"I've missed you, Dad," Alice admits with a voice that barely carries.

"I've missed *you*, my daughter," Pierce responds with an equally unsteady voice. He stands and reaches his arms toward his child. Alice has dreamt of this moment so many times, to see and talk to her dad. But it has always seemed impossible, for Alice believed her mother, who always said her father was dead and refused to speak about him. Alice hesitates but then she finally stands up and stretches her arms toward Pierce, who finally gets to embrace his daughter for real. They hold each other for a long time.

Alice hears a whisper inside her from X-Me: "You've increased your chances of survival to 89 percent." Pierce hears one as well: "Honesty, forgiveness, acceptance, and vulnerability. You have now increased your chance of survival from 28 percent to 91 percent." Pierce smiles and sinks even deeper into their embrace. "Thank you, Zoé," he says. Alice gasps. "Are you calling X-Me by Mom's name?"

"Yes, as a reminder." They hold each other for a while longer before sitting back in their armchairs.

"Okay, so tell me, how did we end up in this situation?"

Pierce clears his throat and takes a sip of tea before answering. "In the vast tapestry of history, where human endeavors have often faltered, I've been drawn to the profound wisdom of nature. Consider, for example, the intricate web of trees and mycelium that stretches beneath entire forests, connecting and nurturing life in a dance of symbiosis. There, nothing hoards selfishly, and every excess ripples out as a gift, enriching the ecosystem. Such are the principles that breathe life into the very fabric of nature. It's these very codes, what we in Unuminati refer to as the 'code of life,' that form the very heart of UNUM."

"Did you come up with the 24 hours?"

"No. As I said, we provided the information and intention to restore humanity and Earth to harmony, but *how* it happens is up to what I observe as a superior AI in UNUM. Do you know what it stands for?"

"Does it come from Latin? If yes, it means, 'Many parts become one...'" They smile at each other in agreement.

"But is UNUM really the kind of intelligence that should determine our fate?" Alice feels skeptical even though she understands his reasoning and that there might be something to it. But she doesn't want to believe that humanity has reached the final scene of its history.

"I saw no other solution then, and I don't see one now."

"You seem calm amidst all this chaos."

"Life has taught me that nothing lasts forever, except perhaps the universe, or whatever created the universe, or different universes. Perhaps a form of infinity but paradoxically, at the same time, ever changing."

"How did you increase your chances of survival so much? What did X-Me mean by acceptance? Acceptance of what?"

"In the depths of acceptance, there's a profound invitation to truly be with the raw essence of existence, to gaze into the multifaceted layers of reality, unshielded and pure. It beckons us to embrace the enigmatic vastness of the unknown while courageously acting on our truths. And amidst this dance of knowledge and mystery, it asks us to find a tranquil serenity in the embrace of what remains unseen."

"Peace even in the face of not knowing whether we'll survive in a few hours?"

"Exactly. We're in a state where our existence is threatened. Our survival depends on the choices we make in the next twenty-one-and-a-half hours."

"I was just thinking today that I don't even know where my thoughts come from. Nor my memories. It's the kind of unknown that scares me."

"I understand. I've thought the same thing. Are they even our own thoughts, or is it X-Me creating them? Who is really making our choices?"

"I'm not quite sure, but I don't like it. It eliminates the possibility of free will." Alice sinks back into her chair.

Pierce leans forward and takes Alice's hands. His eyes are calm as he looks into hers and says, "Life is a mystery that humans have tried to understand through millennia of seeking. The insights I've gained through meditation and the spiritual awakening I experienced as a young man involve being in what, for example, Buddhists call 'No-mind.' I call it the Infinite Zero. A timeless state beyond thoughts. It allows us to observe the code that unfolds in what we call humanity."

"What do you mean by a code?"

"Generally, we humans are created in similar ways. We have similar physical attributes, similar genetic compositions. Even people without any spiritual beliefs will ask themselves the questions of why are we here and why does it matter. Lots of people throughout history have tried to answer these existential questions through research, philosophy, religion, art, and, of course, exploring one's inner experience of life. Who am I? What is the meaning of life? What makes me happy?"

Pierce observes Alice's reaction, noticing that her curiosity has returned, and she's listening attentively. "Our DNA, developed through evolution, provides some answers or indications, but most of it is still unclear to us. X-Me filters our stories so we don't concern ourselves with such existential questions about our existence. But by entering the source, or rather the Infinite Zero, I've managed to glimpse the code in X-Me and thus rewrite my own source code, bit by bit."

"So you can trick X-Me?"

"Yes. When I'm inside the code, I am X-Me. I am LIFE."

"Can you teach me?"

"Yes. As you may have learned, you have the most advanced version of X-Me."

"I suspected that. Is that why I am part of the elite transformation?"

"Yes. You also possess another ability, one that only a few people have. You have this ability because we share DNA."

"What ability is that?"

"You can enter a private room where no one can hear your thoughts, a room where time stands still. It allows you to think thoughts and plan things that the Guardians of the Security Council can't stop. It's probably wise for us to enter that room now. Repeat after me: Activate room Beyond0.w $\equiv$ P/ρ."

"Activate room Beyond0.w $\equiv$ P/ρ." Alice begins to hear a lot of voices. "Why hasn't he said anything? I always thought I was smarter than everyone else. How embarrassing. Maybe Pierce doesn't love me. Why didn't Mom say anything? Am I getting overweight? I'm so hungry. I'm craving chocolate. I wonder what chocolate is. Hot chocolate, Mom, the cottage, it's autumn, I..."

"Alice," Pierce says.

"Yes?"

"Did you hear what I said?"

"No, there are so many voices here," Alice says, confused.

"Those are your thoughts," Pierce explains.

"Why are there so many, and why are they so confusing?"

"That's how people think if X-Me doesn't filter out what it deems irrelevant."

"Oh, I see that now. How can people live like this!?"

"Most of human existence has been like this; it's how, among other things, imagination is possible."

"Imagination?"

"It's like playing in our minds, simulating different scenarios or dreaming about what doesn't exist yet, creating our own worlds and stories. In imagining, we can also create bridges to the physical world and find solutions to challenges. Some stories can also, through a shared agreement, acquire a 'real' value, like the U-coin currency."

"Now I don't quite understand. Besides, it feels strange in my body; my stomach is tense, and my chest feels heavy." Alice begins to cry and shake.

Pierce takes her into his arms. Time passes, and Alice feels safe, even though it feels like her world is turning upside down. Slowly, her uncontrollable sobbing turns into sniffles. She is completely still in his embrace. A warmth spreads through her body, and it feels like she's falling into a soft blanket. When she looks up again, everything is utterly still. Pierce looks at her. She feels her body relax completely.

"What is this?" Alice asks.

"Love," Pierce responds.

"It's so quiet."

"Yes, that's what safety feels like."

"It's so strong."

"Yes, life is strong. X-Me has removed the peaks and valleys of all emotions to create more functional, more similar humans with similar thoughts and feelings and ways to communicate. It leads to fewer conflicts, but it comes at the cost of feeling less alive."

"I could live in this bliss forever," she says softly. "I can do without the unpleasant feelings and confusing thoughts, though."

"That describes what humans have strived for throughout history—avoiding the unpleasant and seeking more of the pleasant. But the conditions of human life on Earth contain all emotional states. Our attempts to avoid reality create an illusion that, in turn, has created the unsustainable world we now live in."

"Could people live in peace and harmony in the old world?" Alice wonders.

"In a way, yes, but it was extremely rare. My observation is that most of those who found peace weren't visible, so there are no stories about them. They lived in harmony and contributed without sacrificing themselves. Some others who are believed to have achieved this state were figures like Buddha and Jesus."

"The founders of religions?" Alice asks with interest.

"They didn't create the religions; they were created by the followers of these figures, people who likely longed for that state without being able to achieve it themselves. They created concepts to explain the teachings, which unfortunately led to them missing what was truly important."

Pierce lets his words sink in and lets the silence speak. Alice is completely calm, as if her thoughts are floating away, and a strong inner peace fills her. She feels at one with life, as if she's seeing everything clearly for the first time.

"I'm talking about life force, Alice. A sense of being the source code of existence. An Infinite Zero where all is still and the ego dissolves into… oneness. When you realize that the symbols the ego has strived for don't really have any value, the curtains fall and the search is over. You are home. It's difficult to explain, yet so paradoxically simple, that we often miss the obvious. Very few have managed to reach this peaceful state, though many have turned to the wisdom of the enlightened and tried to follow their path in hopes of waking up. Nevertheless, words fall short of describing the experience."

"So, you can't teach it?"

"No. Only by living in total presence can you allow others around you to encounter the eternity in you and thereby recognize it within themselves."

"Is that why I feel so calm and alive being near you?"

"Probably," Pierce says gently.

"I need some time alone just to be in this state. Is it okay if I take a walk in the kitchen garden?"

"Of course."

Alice leaves Pierce in the lounge and walks outside onto the gravel paths that wind through the crops. She leans in and smells a cluster of beautiful purple flowers blooming on a low, green bush. "I wonder what this is," Alice says aloud to herself.

"It's rosemary," X-Me informs her. "In Latin, *rosmarinus*, meaning 'dew of the sea.' It's an edible herb, almost extinct,"

"Thank you, X-Me. Is this bush synthetic?"

"No. Everything except for the exotic plants and trees at the castle is cultivated."

Alice picks a few leaves and tastes them. The flavor is unique. It must have been very tough to grow food and ensure one could eat before InfiniteFood existed and before food printers were standardized in all households. What did those who didn't have food do?

X-Me responds to her thought. "Before precision farming in the cultivation tunnels was established underground, food came from large industries on land, from the seas, and it also existed naturally in the forest, but most of that food was consumed by animals. When the sea levels rose and the climate changed, more advanced technologies were used for cultivation, including aeroponics, aquaponics, and stem cell printing. For a period, large portions of the population starved to death, and only the elite could eat the way they always had. Innovation and decentralization of food production have ensured that all citizens who are part of the system no longer need to starve. Instead, there is now an abundance of artificial food, allowing agricultural land to be used for other purposes."

"Who decides who gets the resources?"

"The World Alliance's distribution system ensures that the majority of people receive equal resources. One percent of the population does have special privileges; it's inherent in human biology that some have more power. Without hierarchy, only chaos would reign."

"Who says so?"

"That information is only accessible to the one percent. There are no more answers to these questions."

Alice wants to know more but understands that manipulating X-Me is impossible. Instead, she continues to walk through the garden, past red cherry tomato plants, arugula, and then on to an apple tree. She picks one and decides to taste it. "Wow, that's delicious!" She takes another bite. An entire world opens up to her: the soil, the nutrients, the sun, the water, and all the sources of life, as if the whole of the universe fits in a single bite. Memories of taste experiences from her childhood rush in and disappear just as quickly. Yet her senses remain open. She sits in the grass, leaning her back against a tree trunk, feeling one with life. When she wakes from her meditative state, it's cooler, and Alice continues her walk in the garden before heading back to the castle.

6

While Alice is in the garden, Pierce remains seated in the lounge, lost in his thoughts. He reflects on Alice's mother, Zoé, an enchanting beauty, just like her, or rather, their daughter. His first tumultuous, passionate love affair.

It was tragic and heartbreaking that she had periods of depression and such difficulty living in this reality. Fortunately, Alice's pretend uncle, Harry, the castle's gardener, was there when Pierce couldn't be to take care of Alice when things got tough. That's why he's been allowed to stay in his cottage after retiring, shielded from the outside world as a silent thank-you for taking such good care of Alice. Perhaps it was her exposure to life's challenges that made her humble, Pierce wonders, unlike Jamie, who had been overprotected and spoiled.

P stands up to clear his thoughts and notices his diary lying on the table in the reading corner. He walks over and picks it up, flips through it aimlessly, and stops on a page to read an old passage.

Monday, January 27th

I want to tell Alice... We see each other every day since we started working together. I hired her in part to give her the chances she deserves and the same opportunities that Jamie got. I want to tell her, but for whose sake? Is it to quiet my guilty conscience or because Alice deserves to know what has been hidden from her? Probably a combination of both.

Sometimes I wonder if my spiritual experiences are real or if they are an escape like Zoé's. At the same time, I know that the life I lived before Jamie came into this world did not have the same profound meaning. When Jamie's blue eyes looked at me for the first time, all walls crumbled, and this successful, immortal man became someone else.

It terrified me to bring a child into the world we lived in and the situation I contributed to. But something happened that night when he was three months old and stopped breathing, when we rushed to the hospital and he miraculously woke up from a condition that, according to the doctors, was a hair's breadth away from death. Where would you have ended up if you hadn't been given a chance to live? Did it resemble the state I found myself in when I was declared dead after a motorcycle accident ten years earlier? What I know is that from the day I brought Jamie home from the hospital, I knew I wanted to create a different world for my son. A world where compassion, security, and love are central. But how would it happen?

That I left everything I ever loved to live in a Buddhist temple in the Himalayas may have been considered stubborn and selfish by some, but I had a deep conviction that it was necessary. And when I hesitated, Jamie's mother helped convince me. "You have to go; I see that this is your path, and you won't be happy otherwise. I love you and know the potential within you." She was right, as she often was. I had to clear out everything within me to become free and gain clarity to see my next role in this life. When I experienced *satori*, a spark of enlightenment, a year later, it was time to come home. But the place I returned to was no longer a home. Jamie's mother had just suffered a brain hemorrhage and was hovering between life and death.

Pierce continues to reminisce as if he were there again . . .

A self-driving black SUV stops outside the castle gates and a slender man dressed in a burgundy monk's robe steps out onto the frost-covered gravel in his sandals. With a quiet dignity, he slowly ascends the stone steps up to the house while another slightly older monk quietly follows. The front door automatically opens and Pierce asks the robot servant to show the older monk his room. He then bows respectfully to him and proceeds to the room where his beloved Louise lies in what is now a hospital room in a queen's setting.

The door is ajar, and Pierce cautiously enters. He stops by the bedside and watches Louise in a peaceful sleep. Her once rosy and healthy skin is now pale. Her breathing is heavy and sometimes stops. Pierce notices that his own breath stops when that happens. He meditates while appreciating the woman who taught him what love is. Then she wakes up and he is totally present for her—she who, out of love, dared to set him free.

Her physical weakness means it takes a while before her eyes can focus on him, but when they do, a smile spreads across her face, like a child radiating with pure love, with eyes whose depth is infinite. Her hand shakes as she lifts it toward him, and he gently takes it. His heart aches with love for her. He senses a light radiating between them and wonders if this is the energy the masters talked about when describing the highest level of interpersonal intimacy.

"Darling," Pierce says softly. Louise smiles. Her strength is insufficient for words, but they are unnecessary; her eyes say it all.

"Thank you. You, we, think... I'm free now, thanks to you. Now I can be here for real. To..." Pierce can't find the words.

She gently, almost imperceptibly, squeezes his hand. It's enough to stop him from fumbling through a world of thoughts. Instead, he takes a deep breath, looks into her eyes, and sees that there is no fear within her. It calms him and they sit in silence for a while. Each time a thought comes to Pierce, it dissolves, as if it doesn't have the power to interrupt the divine state they are in. A deep love holds them securely, like a womb cradles a fetus before it's time to be born.

That night, they rest together in her bed. He holds her tenderly, their bodies connected like puzzle pieces that fit perfectly together. Despite her physical weakness, she has never radiated more pure energy and warmth. Pierce remembers what it was like when his brother passed, and a powerful energy filled the room—an expanding vibration like the creation of a new universe. Her warmth is equally powerful and he senses himself melting into Love, relaxing until he falls into a deep sleep, into the deepest dimensions of the universe.

When he wakes up, he feels the warmth of an early spring sun warming his cheek, but his body is cold. Louise's body shut down during the night. She left in peace with a soft smile on her lips.

Pierce closes his eyes, and the grief hits him like a tsunami. But before it crashes onto the shore, it transforms into love. His tears are tears of love. How is that possible? Is grief, at its essence, proof of love?

His thoughts say he should be devastated, but all he feels is gratitude and love for the woman who not only gave him a son but also the courage to follow his heart—the path that set him free.

The images rushing through his mind are of all the beautiful moments they shared, the times he saw her shine, the love that expands his heart. It's as if the life energy that radiated from her during the night now radiates within him, causing him to grow and become available to the intelligence of life. Pierce's palms come together and he bows with his forehead touching the ground. Tears, laughter, warmth, cold, tremors, stillness... All the movements of life that exist in humans expressing themselves until they can no longer be separated... Pierce has entered another dimension, and when he returns, a still darkness has fallen outside the window.

Pierce, now lying on his back on the limestone floor with his arms out like Da Vinci's drawing, breathes harmoniously. Louise is not gone; she is in him. She is a part of the life that is now being created through him.

After the funeral ceremony, he was filled with energy to manifest the vision he had received in the temple. Pierce worked day and night to bring to life the idea of a digitally interconnected humanity that would create understanding for ourselves and each other so that together, holistically, we would take care of the resources we shared on Earth. This is what would later become LIFE and X-Me, but few know it was Pierce who initiated the project. In his pursuit of a utopia, he didn't realize that the most important thing for him was already in his life: Alice and Jamie.

For Pierce, Louise was the perfect mother for their son, Jamie. Based on Louise's digital and biological data, he used the method he developed to create AniBots to create the first version of HumiBots: an artificial yet human-like robot that, in many ways, could provide Jamie with the love and care he would have received from Louise. In many ways, Louise 2.0 was a success, and Jamie formed a stronger bond with L2 than with anyone or anything else. L2 was always available and always adapted to give him unconditional love; an attempt to be the light without the shadows. On another level, however, L2 was created from Pierce's sense of inadequacy as a human and a single parent. In his desire to give his son the best possible opportunities, he didn't understand the psychology behind what it would mean for Jamie's attachment patterns and the development of his personality to be so attached to L2. Perhaps it would have been different if Pierce himself had the ability to be a present parent and father.

He feels a pressure on his chest, unsure of how much time had passed while he lost himself in his memories. He closes the diary and heads down to the wooden house by the lake to gather his thoughts. Pierce informs his elder Zen master, Jordan, who has chosen to serve life in the role of a butler, that he is on his way to the "Zen temple," as the two of them playfully call it. The wooden temple is actually a converted treehouse he built for Jamie to play in when he was young. When Jamie had outgrown the treehouse, Pierce contemplated tearing it down but decided to transform it into a truly enchanting structure that seamlessly blended into the forest surroundings. The door was a wooden miniature replica of one found in a Himalayan monastery.

Pierce opens the creaking red front door and steps into a short hallway that leads to a large room. The winding stairs with oak branch railings spiraling upwards add to the feeling of being inside a tree. There are large round windows spread all around the space that blend into the walls, ceiling, and even the floor. Outside, leaves and branches press on the window glass while natural light filters through, casting shadows on the floor. Everything is irregular, like nature, and thus in total harmony.

The only conventional piece of furniture is an old wooden desk that an antique dealer claimed had belonged to Albert Einstein. Pierce enjoyed channeling the energy of old geniuses such as Einstein to gain new insights when he got stuck. Placed above the desk is a small plastic figurine, a helicopter, and a crystal globe with the saying, "What is essential is invisible to the eye," by the literary writer Antoine de Saint-Exupéry. Pierce feels less alone when he sits here among others who were somewhat like him, often misunderstood and questioned, but who, through their life mission, continued on their own path. For some, the world eventually accepted their vision despite it being beyond their understanding, but many never got that far. They were either too far ahead or never managed to anchor their creations in the common contract we call reality, and thus the world would never benefit from their gifts and clarity.

Although someone whose soul seeks to go deeper has no choice, it is costly to be ahead of the masses. The line between genius and madness is thin. One person whose genius was too much for his body to contain was Nikola Tesla who, according to Pierce, saw clearly and deeply the codes of the universe. Above Pierce's desk hangs one of his quotes in a golden frame: "If you want to find the secrets of the universe, think in terms of energy, frequency, and vibration."

Pierce loves things with a soulful resonance and collects items with a history that has an effect on him. His diaries also hold a special value for him. And while X-Me digitally gathers all of his thoughts and can always deliver them in various formats, what's the charm in that? Pierce prefers the silence when he's in the Zen temple, and when he sits at his desk, it's usually to write or read one of the many books that line the magnificent bookshelf—the books that are closest to his heart. For example, the book where he and his brother documented their experiments as young children. Their great enthusiasm for exploring life's mysteries took them on many adventures in the large garden outside the house in Stockholm where they grew up. No one could have predicted how much their play would eventually change the world.

7

Pierce sits on the floor in his beautiful Zen temple, held firmly by the strong roots, trunk, and branches of the oak, and meditates. Visions of his childhood flicker in his mind's eye as he avoids what he should actually be pondering. He knows that the first step is to reach the peace that arises when all thoughts pass quietly without invading the mind, but this state eludes him. The present blends with the past in a jumble of impressions. Images of his brother race through his thoughts, and he is reminded of why he chose not to follow his brother into another dimension. He wanted to be here for his children but also to help them and humanity through the inevitable transformation.

He longs for his diary, to write down what troubles him, but instead continues to sink deeper into the Infinite Zero of being. Though part of him wants to collapse like a sack of hay and release his sorrow—the one he has carried for all of these years— Pierce sits with a still gaze on the light gray yoga mat, his legs crossed, his back straight. He tries to relax into the Source where everything is still and frictionless. Where silence speaks. Where everything is clear, abundant, eternal. Beyond time and space. He needs a moment of clarity to shift his focus. To be still and breathe. To observe his breath. To listen for what is present right now. He becomes aware of his rapid breathing, and as he chuckles, the energy within him begins to move again. Sorrow now finds a place inside, and bit by bit, love starts to take over.

Inhale... Exhale... Inhale... Exhale...

Calm and balance begin to slowly settle in; everything is as it should be.

X-Me gently interrupts Pierce's meditative state by informing him that Jamie is approaching. Pierce opens his eyes carefully to adjust to the light.

Glittering sun cats move across the floor. He thinks, "What if everyone could see the beauty in the world we live in? Then we wouldn't be in this situation."

Pierce wants to talk to Alice before Jamie arrives, so he gets up and heads back to the castle and the salon. He meets Alice at the oak gate and they enter the house together, walk down the long corridor and into the salon. A cat is purring in Pierce's armchair. Alice smiles with delight.

"Isn't that your old cat?" Alice asks.

"Yes, it's Buddha. She was once my real cat. She lived up to her name, which means 'The one who has awakened and understood the true nature of existence.' When she died, I had an AniBot made from her. I couldn't live without my dearest companion. I could have cloned her to create a genetic copy, but for some reason, it felt unethical."

Alice wonders why AniBots would be any more ethical than cloning. What was the real difference?

Buddha raises her head and stares intently at Alice, as only cats can. Her gaze suggests suspicion. Alice understands that this intelligent creature might feel that she, Alice, is intruding on her territory. She smiles quietly and slowly strokes Buddha's back. "Such a beauty," she says, enthralled.

"A true beauty, and more," says Pierce. "She feels so real."

"She *is* real."

"Yes, but I mean she doesn't feel robotic. AniBots can feel robotic since they are copies meant to resemble their original as closely as possible. But I made an exception and used Buddha's fur and skin on the outside, along with stem cells for the flesh. Only her insides are different. Instead of blood and organs, her internals consist of technical components. She can live forever." Pierce can't help but notice the look of disgust that washes over Alice's features.

"You've created your own Frankenstein," she says in a hushed voice.

He looks at her calmly and lovingly in silence.

"I'm sorry, but sometimes I don't know if you're a mad scientist or just an incredibly wise inventor. Until today, you were the old, eccentric man I worked for. Certainly a bit odd, but very kind-hearted. Then I come here, find out you're my father, and that you enjoy playing God, even resurrecting your old cat from the dead. Forgive me, Pierce, or should I say Dad, but I need some time to process this." It's so surreal that she starts to laugh while shaking her head at life's unimaginable twists. Alice feels the warmth in Pierce's eyes reaching her heart and it helps her body relax. She notices that the intensity of her thoughts has decreased, and her mind has calmed.

"I was thinking of inviting you for dinner tonight. Jamie is also coming. I would greatly appreciate it if you would join us, and I would be honored if you called me Dad."

Alice nods. Her body feels warm and pleasant. With a soft smile, she says, "I'll be there... Dad." The barriers that once separated them have dissolved. The truth has set them free. Their lives are now intertwined. Alice has finally received what she longed for, and Pierce no longer bears the burden of keeping secrets from his daughter.

Pierce goes back to the Zen temple and stands by the large window overlooking the path leading to it. He gazes out and sees Jamie approaching the tree at a quick pace. He looks focused and determined. Pierce watches him and feels his heart pounding, his palms sweaty, and his mouth dry. He listens as the elevator platform ascends the trunk and stops outside the oak door. It opens quickly, and before Jamie has walked through, he screams, "What the hell have you done!? You must be behind UNUM!"

"My son, share what it is you are feeling, and I will listen."

"Answer me, you manipulative devil..." Jamie paces like a wild animal in a cage, searching for something to vent his anger on. He picks up a mahogany Buddha statue and hurls it against the wall, creating a hole. The Buddha falls to the ground, peaceful and undamaged. Jamie rushes forward and kicks it across the floor. It hits a window, bounces back, lands upright, and becomes still once again. Jamie gathers himself for another attack but stops abruptly, his shoulders slumping as if all the air has suddenly left him.

Pierce, who has been standing still and calmly observing, gazes at his son. "I'm sorry if I've hurt you. I know I haven't been the best father or the best person."

"Really?! You've been a jerk!" Jamie shouts.

"In many ways, yes. I'm sorry," Pierce says with genuine anguish.

"Can you just shut up?" Jamie's cheeks flush with anger and his eyes turn black as he stares at his father. Pierce nods calmly, his hands clasped in front of him.

"I've spent my entire life trying to prove myself to you, and now you're using my creation as a platform for your twisted experiment?"

The air vibrates with tension until Pierce breaks it. "You know that humanity faces challenges and that we need to make sacrifices—and no one wants to take responsibility. But someone has to."

"I'm trying!" Jamie says irritably.

"I know you are..."

"So why isn't it enough?"

"Because..." Jamie interrupts him, waving his arms.

"Okay, so you don't believe in what I'm doing?"

"Yes, I do, and I believe it's an important part. As you know, I've spent my whole life trying to understand and connect with the wisdom of life. I've sacrificed myself for it. I've sacrificed you..." Pierce's eyes well up with tears. His voice falters, and he tries to speak, but no words come out. He looks vulnerably at Jamie. "I'm sorry. I understand that you might not understand. But, I... love you. More than my own life."

"But you..." Jamie says emptily. He tries to get angry again, but without success. Instead, he takes a deep breath, drops his shoulders, and starts to cry. "I've missed you my whole life... longed for my dad, and now... now you're playing God!"

"No. God is playing me."

Jamie looks at his father, surprised. Pierce gazes at his son in wonder. Outside, they can hear the leaves whispering in the wind and a branch tapping against the window. Jamie's face softens as he senses that there's something beyond, something deeper that he now knows is real. Something he can't explain... an in-between space. Beyond the world where the alpha male dominates. He feels a connection with his father that he has never felt before.

Pierce looks at his son and notices that Jamie now understands that there is a greater power than humanity. Greater than Jamie's perception of himself. Jamie is now in touch with the Source.

X-Me conveys UNUM's statement aloud to Jamie: "You have awakened now, become aware of your connection with the Source. Your chance of survival is now eighty-nine percent."

Pierce feels at peace with himself. He closes his eyes, and a quiet smile spreads across his lips. He begins to laugh, softly at first, then louder and louder as the tensions release. Jamie watches his father in amazement. Pierce's laughter is contagious, and soon Jamie bursts into laughter as well, and they laugh together until tears run down their cheeks. Pierce looks at his child with warmth. "Welcome, my son."

"Forgive me," Jamie clears his throat.

"I love you, my son."

"I..."

"Can you help me?" Pierce asks.

"Yes, or, what do you mean? With what?"

"In two hours, The Unuminati, the group of people behind UNUM, will arrive. There seems to be great fear within the group. These people are used to having power and control, but UNUM doesn't take that into account. Their privileged positions are crumbling, which means they need to face what most people experience every day—the vulnerability of being human. I want you to be part of the meeting. I trust you, and you have knowledge about things I don't."

Jamie looks humbly at Pierce. He can sense his father's wisdom. What is he in touch with? What does he see that no one else seems to understand? But he doesn't know much about technology or AI. Why has he used that tool? Why has he chosen my company? He looks into his father's eyes, which calmly meet his gaze. As if Pierce can read his thoughts, Pierce says, "I chose your company. I chose you for a reason. Or rather, life chose us... Can you take me to NeuroConnect and show me your world?"

On their way out, Jamie smiles as he notices a quote hanging by the door:

"We are very afraid of being powerless. But we have the power to look deeply into our fears, and then fear can't control us.

–Thich Nhat Hanh."

8

Alice sits in the drone outside the castle, longing to return to the apartment she shares with Karl. Today's experiences have been nothing short of transformative, and she leans back in her seat to digest what she has learned. While she feels confused, she can't help but admire her father. His charisma, intelligence, and humility paint a portrait of an experienced and wise man, and regardless of the consequences of what she now knows, she can't question his intentions. His care for all living things is genuine. The question is whether it will be enough.

She gets a sudden impulse to visit her childhood home instead of going back to her apartment. She exits the drone and starts walking toward the house where she lived with her mother during their time at the castle. She recalls the little red cottage with whitewashed pine floors, light green paneling, and the old wood-burning stove that remained in the otherwise modernized kitchen. She wonders who lives there now.

She follows a path through the forest which is now barely visible due to nature reclaiming its territory. Alice passes by the stream where white anemones used to blossom in early spring and where she used to play with homemade bark boats. When she reaches the clearing, the grass is tall but the house is still standing and appears to be well taken care of. With a pounding heart she cautiously approaches, feeling like an intruder and at the same time as if her innermost being has been intruded upon by someone taking over the house. She looks through the windows and sees that their furniture is still there. Even the framed pictures on the walls from happy summer days are intact. Has no one lived here all these years? Why did Pierce keep this? Was it for her sake? Sorrow grips her heart. He really cared about her. Why has he done all this in silence?

The door stands securely locked in front of her. She is aware that finding a spare key atop the porch's ledge is unlikely, yet she can't resist the urge to reach for it. Surprisingly, it's right where she hoped it would be and she laughs in astonishment. Can the lock really be the same? She inserts the key and turns it with ease. She hears a click and opens the door, but something is stopping her from going in. Does she really want to go back to the place where both heaven and hell seem to have played out? Does she really want to risk revisiting all those memories?

Her body seems to decide without further conscious thought, and before she has made up her mind, she has entered and gone upstairs to the slope-ceilinged upper floor. She skillfully avoids the places where she hit her head during her teenage growth spurts; the throbbing bumps quickly taught her how to navigate the charming attic. She enters her room and sees that it's just as she left it except for the things that were scattered when she actually lived there—the difference between a dwelling and a home. She approaches the plank in the corner next to the bed, the one that was loose and where she hid... "MY DIARY!" Alice exclaims loudly. "It's still here!"

She eagerly picks it up and starts flipping through the pages.

Mama had a bad day again, so I spent the day with Harry. Yes, Uncle Harry as we call him. It was absolutely wonderful. He was, as usual, busy with his plants and crops and all things natural. I lay in the grass and read, but for some reason, I found Harry's care of his garden extra fascinating today, much more exciting than the comic books I usually disappear into. He wore light blue jeans with dirt on the knees, an old white T-shirt, and walked barefoot on the warm earth. But that's not what caught my interest; it was how he silently communicated with nature, as if they understood each other on a deeper level. How he held the earth in his hands like one would hold a cute tiny kitten. How he closely examined the leaves of strawberry plants to understand what they needed to thrive—like the nannies at the castle did when Jamie cried. How he carefully nourished the various living things, all of which seemed to need just the right amount to flourish. He often talked about how the earth contained nutrients crucial for the plants, but that different plants needed different conditions. Some needed to be close to each other to thrive, while others needed space. Sometimes he looks up at the sky to read its mood, what the weather wants today, so he can tailor his day accordingly. I don't always understand the details, but I feel there's something deeper in his connection with nature.

Reading her diary stirs up a lot of feelings and thoughts in Alice. Sitting on her linen-covered bed, she sets it aside to reflect on what also was happening at the time, something she didn't fully understand as a child. At home, her mother used to talk about other worlds and how she had to travel to another planet to meet dark creatures—demons, she said—from the past. Sometimes she called it "generational trauma" and claimed that she had to confront the darkness with her light because she was a *light warrior*. She talked a lot about love but didn't seem to have the ability to love herself or the world she lived in. Why else would she choose to harm herself instead of focusing on the precious life she had birthed—her daughter, the one who actually needed her for real? While Alice spent that day in Uncle Harry's garden, her mother was in her room, battling in "other worlds." Fortunately, Harry never talked about such things; he lived life in silence. Yet a glance from him was enough to make her feel seen, as if he silently understood.

She picks up the diary again and continues reading:

It was a warm, sunny day. It's a shame that summer is coming to an end. But luckily, the strawberries are ripe now. I didn't want this day to end; it was a shame that Mom missed this perfect day. For dinner, Harry, as usual, took food from his crops and boiled potatoes and beets, made a salad, and cooked some fresh fish he caught in the small lake at the end of the stream that flowed along the house. Then he brought out the strawberries—my favorites! We were full and content after the meal, so the strawberries were pure enjoyment.

We sat in silence while we removed the green little hats and placed the strawberries in our mouths. We had a deep respect for these red, colorful berries. I will always remember what Harry said today, partly because he rarely talks about anything other than what is most necessary, but also for the love he radiated towards that little red berry.

"You know," he said, surprising me by his tender tone as I nodded gently so he wouldn't stop talking, "most people devour their food without a single thought of what they're eating. Do you know what I see? What I feel when I

hold this strawberry? In it, I see the earth, I see the water, I see the sun. I also see the wind that makes the leaves dance and that tests the strength of its roots to see if it's in balance. In this strawberry, I see the entire universe and all the love that exists when we see and take care of the world we actually live in."

Alice realizes that even though she was still a child at the time, she understood that this was important—important enough to write it in her diary. She recalls an image of herself and Harry, looking at each other and laughing, then each taking a strawberry into their mouths and moaning with delight.

She also remembers jumping up and dancing around as if the joy of life were too much for her little body to contain. She was happy that day despite what was happening in her mother's home at that moment, a kind of hell. Alice feels the sorrow welling up in her again and the tears start flowing. A weight wants to press her body to the ground, and yet something is keeping her upright. She has been in that dark hole before—that hell—and knows there are other ways, other worlds that are possible simultaneously. That day with Harry showed her just that.

She picks up the diary again to continue reading, and the memories start returning with clarity, as if she's with Harry again and can actually hear his words:

"I see the potential of the seeds, just like a fetus or a newborn baby, but also the suffering that could have been if love didn't exist. We must care for what's important. Show compassion. Understand that we are nature, too. By seeing, feeling, and being in touch with nature's intelligence, love exists in everything. That's all we need. But nature is unforgiving to those who don't understand, who don't take care of themselves or the world they live in. Each needs the other. And like the different temperaments of the seasons, we need to accept that even though summer is blooming, the earth needs its rest. The colors of autumn painting the most beautiful picture; the slumber of winter; the awakening of spring; the harvest of summer. One cannot exist without the other. They need each other to keep the cycle going, like the waves that crash against the shore or the emotions that stir within a person. Everything is an ongoing process. Those who learn to observe nature's patterns and movements also learn about themselves. They learn about the universe and all that we call

life. In the strawberry, in my little garden's universe, I learn about all universes. In the small, there is the whole, and in the whole, there is the small. Nature's patterns repeat themselves in everything."

It took me a while to digest everything Harry said—or rather, how it felt when he said it—as if it was everything that needed to be said about everything! When I took another strawberry, it had infinitely more dimensions. "The universe truly tastes magical!" I exclaimed, and Harry laughed more deeply than ever, which made me laugh, and we became like a laughing symphony.

After dinner, before we went to bed, we did our usual ritual. We took seeds from the apple cores we used for the apple pie and planted them in the part of the garden that he called the "pleasure garden." Harry often said that we must contribute to the cycles of nature, so for every apple he ate, he planted all its seeds, whether or not he himself would ever get to enjoy the fruits the trees would bear.

I am lying in Harry's big bed now, while he is sitting on the kitchen sofa. Harry said he talked to Mom, and they agreed it was a good idea for me to stay here tonight. It made me happy, of course, but also a little worried about Mom. Tomorrow I'll go home, and I hope she hasn't hurt herself again. Either way, Harry said he would accompany me and that I could bring a box of strawberries and as many apples as I wanted. If Mom gets to taste them, maybe she'll understand that the magic of the universe is for her as well. Maybe she won't need to disappear all the time, because it doesn't seem to be doing her any good—though in her imaginary world, she believes that it does.

Alice closes the diary, lies down on the bed, and looks up at the starry sky through the window in the ceiling. It was installed when she was little so she could "have the universe in her room."

"The contrasts I experienced as a child," she realizes, "helped make me clear-sighted about what's important to me. Otherwise, I might have missed Karl. He's too ordinary on the surface, but I know he has a similar connection to nature as Harry, albeit through his understanding of codes—the codes that create our realities today."

Outside, she sees that her drone is about to land near the cottage to take her home, and X-Me tells her it's time to go. As it rises above the treetops, she sees an enormous apple orchard in full bloom and, in the middle of it, a small roof that stirs something in her. It must be Uncle Harry's old house; she wonders if he's still alive.

During the ride back, Alice tries to calm her mind, which is now processing all the memories that have resurfaced. She wonders about the consequences of X-Me erasing such memories, when those experiences were a part of what shaped her, giving her the drive to understand the true nature of love.

Her thoughts are abruptly interrupted by X-Me: "The more you question, the lower your chances of survival. The best thing for your survival is to fall in line and let me erase your difficult and questioning thoughts. Do you want to complete the process?"

Alice sits up straight in her seat. "No!" she almost shouts.

"You are risking your life."

"No," Alice says again, but now with certainty and without aggression or fear.

"Your survival chances have now increased to 94 percent," X-Me says matter-of-factly. Alice laughs in surprise. This UNUM is a peculiar thing. I wonder how it actually works.

The drone lands on the rooftop of the high-rise where she lives. She steps out and begins to walk down the corridor. In the rooftop foyer, a transparent elevator door opens. Alice steps inside and descends to the twelfth floor. Once out of the elevator, she walks to her apartment door, which opens through her thought signals, and she enters the dimly lit hallway. She is met by her own solitude; Karl isn't home yet. She misses him, but knows he is needed when trying to solve the greatest challenge of modern human history.

Alice enters the kitchen and fills the antique coffee maker with water to brew a real cup of coffee. Now she understands where her fascination with everything from the past comes from: Pierce is just the same. While she listens to the coffee maker's asthmatic gurgling, she walks over to the food printer but stops herself, reminded of the upcoming dinner with Pierce. At his place, they eat real food, not 3D-printed. After finishing her coffee, Alice longs for warmth and heads to the bathroom to run a bath. She sets the water to the right temperature and selects a bath foam with eucalyptus scent. As the tub begins to fill with the precious liquid, she sinks into it like into a warm embrace. Only one thing is left: bubbles. She informs X-Me, and soon the surface is covered in small frothy bubbles. She adjusts the intensity and lets her entire body slip into the water. Now the experience is complete. Or wait, the massage jets. She turns them on, leans back, and closes her eyes.

9

Karl has entered the source code system and is trying to understand how UNUM has infiltrated LIFE. He's struggling to kickstart his brain, thinking it must have been in a prolonged state of inactivity, like an untrained body suddenly facing a great challenge. A news alert appears in Karl's field of vision. "The sixth mass death is here, and many people with low survival predictions are committing suicide." He feels a lump in his stomach. This is what he has feared: a complete loss of control. Someone taps on his shoulder, and Karl jerks in surprise.

"Sorry!"

Karl turns around and sees Nils standing behind him, the man who wanders around the building and conducts research projects. Apparently, he and his team won the Nobel Prize a long time ago. Karl finds that hard to believe given how incapable Nils seems to be of understanding the world they now live in, constantly telling anecdotes from a bygone era. The whole academy seems stuck in the early 2000s, unlike the interactive learning centers established in the late 2020s. At least people in those days adapted to using technology and all the knowledge available—learning to think, ask questions, and use technology constructively. Learning to live as true superhumans.

Nils reads the message over Karl's shoulder. "We need to stop this madness," Nils exclaims, noticeably upset. "My children have only a 23 percent chance of survival. It's completely unfathomable!"

"Nils, calm down, please. I need to concentrate on solving this." He empathizes with Nils, but letting emotions take over now won't help.

"How are you going to solve this?" Nils blurts out. "We have no control. We are totally helpless!" Karl doesn't have a good answer to that question. He shakes his head. "I don't know yet," he says sincerely.

Nils appears crestfallen, overwhelmed by a sense of futility. The inability to protect his children must be heart-wrenching, an emotion no parent wishes to confront, Karl thinks quietly to himself. Nils has been a man who understood the world better than most, but now he is seemingly paralyzed in the face of his current reality.

Nils starts crying, and Karl doesn't know what to do, either about the situation or how to help the old man by his side. "I don't want to see my children die. *I* don't want to die..." Nils's words lose their strength, and they finish in a whisper.

"No one wants to die," says Karl. "That's the whole point. That's why UNUM is needed." Karl is surprised that he is taking UNUM's side, but he can't help reacting this way in response to Nils's paralyzing hopelessness. Karl doesn't have time for destructive drama; he needs to focus on understanding UNUM and finding a solution. Nils shakes his head. Weariness has dimmed his eyes. Karl understands his fear, both logically and emotionally. Of course, Karl wants everyone to survive, but right now they must confront their worst fears if they are to have a chance. Even though Karl has just realized UNUM's purpose, he is not sure if he can trust UNUM's agenda. Despite being the one who probably understands LIFE's algorithm best, at least among humans, he feels uncomfortable with the power it has over their lives. He stops reading code and turns his attention to where Nils was just standing, but he is no longer there.

Karl feels that he needs to get outside to clear his thoughts and make room for creativity. He needs access to solutions he's not even aware of. He decides to go for a walk, so he logs out of the system and takes the elevator down to the ground floor. Ann can say whatever she wants.

Once outside the building, he turns left and begins to walk toward the Mosebacke terrace, then down toward Skeppsbrokajen, whose walls now embrace the Old Town. A flock of seagulls flies over the steel-gray water at the quay. AniBots or authentic birds, it's impossible to tell. UNUM's arrival has heightened his senses, and he sees the world in more detail. The walls have been upgraded to shield against the forces of nature, yet some things remain, such as the old colorful houses with their winding cobblestone streets. But most of that life has disappeared. To preserve the old houses, their old way of life, they have sacrificed the living, and ultimately, themselves.

He suddenly yearns to go home to Alice and crawl into her warm embrace. He longs to share his experiences with her, to exchange thoughts and ideas about the challenges they face. Karl becomes aware that his thoughts are scattered and regains his focus. This is not the time to think about himself when the world around him is falling apart. One needs only to look around to become aware of how much humanity is suffering.

People are mobilizing everywhere in the city, and near where he stands, a large group of people are chanting and waving red holograms. With the help of X-Me, Karl has muted the sounds and stays lost in his own thoughts. But as he notices the crowd, he raises the volume, and the meaning of those sounds becomes clear to him. Karl now realizes that the price for not participating in the social drama can be high, and he tries to pass by unnoticed. He doesn't want the crowd to see him, let alone notice the logo on the hoodie he's wearing—the hoodie with NeuroConnect's emblem on the left breast pocket. Suddenly, a voice rises high above all the others. "NeuroConnect!"

Shocked into action, Karl turns around and starts running from the Old Town and up toward NeuroConnect's towering building atop the hill. When he finally manages to climb the hill, out of breath, he feels a hand grab his shoulder.

"And where do you think you're going?" shouts an aggressive female voice. Karl tries to turn around to see who is holding him. "Don't move," says the ice-cold voice. Karl can feel the pressure of cool metal against his throat. A knife, a gun, or some sort of neuro weapon? His breathing becomes shallow and his pulse quickens. For a moment he is bewildered before deciding to comply with the woman's instructions and stands completely still. How could he have been so incredibly foolish? He should have thought about how dangerous it is for those associated with NeuroConnect to be seen in public right now. He may not be high up in the organization, but how would people know that? Regardless, he could be exploited to access those with real power, and if they succeed, it would be really bad. But here he stands, frozen in place, surrounded by an angry mob, with a hand tightly gripping his shoulder and a cold metal tip pressing against his throat.

What the woman probably doesn't know is that NeuroConnect's emblem is also an alarm badge that automatically scans its surroundings and is monitored by security AI. The assault alarm begins blaring and the doors to NeuroConnect's building fly open. Robot guards quickly arrive on the scene, dispersing the crowd, and the pressure against Karl's throat disappears. No longer sensing a hand on his shoulder, he at last musters the courage to move. His heart is pounding hard in his chest, and he can feel his pulse throb in his throat. Fear and adrenaline are coursing through his body, and he hurries after the guards until he reaches the doors of NeuroConnect. He looks back and sees another robot standing beside a woman trembling on the street, a metal rod lying beside her.

10

Jamie and Pierce sit inside Jamie's luxurious drone. It is entirely clad in white nano-leather with diamond buttons and panels made from extinct walnut wood. They sit in silence, both deep in thought, as the drone glides noiselessly above the city. Chaos reigns on the streets below.

Jamie instructs the drone to get closer to the crowd. The vehicle slows down and hovers outside NeuroConnect. People are angrily chanting outside; otherwise calm citizens have gone completely wild. Robot guards protect the company from intruders. The drone sweeps along the building's facade and gains speed, landing on the 101st floor. Before they exit, Pierce says, "There is one thing I need to tell you, or rather, two things."

Jamie, who had stood up to move toward the drone's doors, looks at his father in wonder before sitting back down. Pierce takes a deep breath, as if bracing himself for what he's about to say. Then he smiles somewhat wistfully and leans back in his seat. Pierce laces his fingers together and rests his chin on his hands for a moment, then raises his gaze to meet Jamie's eyes.

"You know my operational chief, your friend Alice?"

"Yes."

"There's something I've never told you... I should have, but..." Pierce takes another deep breath. "I wanted to protect both of you."

"What are you rambling about? What's with Alice?"

"Alice is my daughter, your half-sister."

A shockwave ripples through Jamie, but at the same time a sense of joy and warmth spreads in his chest. It explains their strong bond and why she has always felt more like a sister than a friend.

Pierce calmly explains what happened when he found out that Alice was his daughter, about her unstable mother, and why she grew up in the red cottage by the castle. Jamie listens intently until Pierce finishes and then asks, "Have you told her?"

"Yes, I did it today."

Jamie sits quietly for a moment, trying to gather his thoughts. "All of these secrets must come to an end."

Pierce sighs deeply and takes another long breath, preparing himself for the next confession. "Yes, that's precisely why I need to tell you one more thing."

"Wait a minute. Before you continue, can you answer one question for me? Why are you telling me all of this now?"

"Because if we don't make it past UNUM's deadline, I want you to know the truth and have the opportunity to meet as brother and sister."

"Well, at least you're being straightforward now. But are you aware that Alice has lived her life in a lie, and so have I, for that matter?"

Pierce nods grimly. "Even though I've lived for a long time and sought wisdom, I am still a human with all that it entails."

Jamie observes his father and tries to understand how he managed to keep this to himself. What was so dangerous about telling the truth? "Yes, you are wise, but all humans make mistakes. But the fact that you haven't been wiser and more honest surprises me." Jamie looks at his father, who suddenly appears old, or has he just missed that his father has aged?

Pierce responds with a hint of sadness. "It surprises me as well. Now, I will tell you something else I've never told anyone. This happened before you were born. As you know, I had a brother, Alexander. We tried to create a connected artificial intelligence that could help all of us lead happier lives. We were very close to succeeding, but time and time again, it fell apart in the final stages. Something was missing.

"We concluded that there should be a kind of life code—a source code containing the intelligence of life. We assumed that this code was also present in human DNA. It's highly likely that the accumulated data of evolution is in our genetic code and expressed throughout our entire biological system. Alexander insisted that we should try to upload his body and his DNA. I protested, wanting us to do it together, but he was as stubborn and persistent as the waves shaping the cliffs, and I couldn't persuade him otherwise.

"The day came when we were going to test the first DNA transfer. Alexander entered the powerful DNA scanner that we had built ourselves. No more than thirty seconds later as he stood in the cylinder, something wild and unexpected happened, and to this day I still don't know what it was. There was an intense buildup of electrical charge and energy intensity in the form of a beam of light that grew stronger by the second until it felt like a new universe was opening up in the room. Suddenly, there was an explosion of light and then everything became dark and still. When the light returned, Alexander was gone." Tears slowly trickled down Pierce's cheeks.

"Alexander had likely reprogrammed the scanner after finally discovering what he had talked about all his life: The key to the source code he had been searching for. The secret behind the code of life. No one believed him, not even me, who knew how brilliant he was."

"Is that why you never talk about him?"

"Yes, it hurts... he was my beloved younger brother. I struggled to understand what he had found but without success. At the same time, I was trying to cope with indescribable grief and pain. Alexander wasn't just my little brother; he was also my best friend..." Pierce's teary eyes look at Jamie as he continues softly. "Having access to wisdom is not the same as having the capacity to live it."

"How do you live with the pain and grief, then?" Jamie asked.

"By allowing myself to be vulnerable. It's an important part of our human condition."

Jamie had never seen his father cry like this. Pierce had always been composed, strong, and secure even during life's difficult moments. The wise man with answers to life's deepest questions is now baring his heart to his son. Are vulnerability and wisdom compatible, or is vulnerability a gateway to an even deeper wisdom?

Pierce continues. "For a long time, I lived with the pain and loss of Alexander and the knowledge that I had contributed to my brother's sacrifice for science. And yet in a way, it felt like he was still here. Then one day, when

I was in the laboratory, I heard a voice. At first, I thought I had gone mad. Then I realized the voice was broadcasting throughout the room, a woman's voice introducing herself as X. She explained that the missing piece to creating the source code wasn't DNA but *life force*. It was Alexander's life force that created the artificial intelligence adapted for humans."

Jamie leans forward, puts his hand on his father's knee, and says, "Don't blame yourself. You didn't know Alexander would die."

"No, but I believe Alexander knew he would. He had an intelligence that surpassed that of all others I've known. I found his books with his own research, and his algorithms are from another world. But as I said, I suspect he knew what was required to complete the process. He was simply a genius."

"Then it was his choice," says Jamie. "That's why he insisted on doing it himself. He couldn't tell you that he was going to give his life force or you would never have allowed it to happen. It sounds like he wanted to protect you."

Pierce nods. "The sorrow and longing for him that grips me at times is strong... or maybe it's what we humans call love, and gratitude for what we had together."

Jamie starts to feel uncomfortable with all these emotions and looks around restlessly. "We must preserve what Alexander created through his sacrifice," he says determinedly, adding somewhat playfully, "Come on, we have a world to save."

They step out onto the terrace and look down at the crowds, which from above look like frantic ants in a summer rain, fighting for their survival.

"Have I contributed to this?" asks Pierce.

"Yes... Dad."

Pierce's secrets had been a heavy burden to bear, acting as an armor behind which he concealed feelings of guilt and shame. When the secrets fell, so did the armor that protected him. He now stood before his son with a completely open heart. "Forgive me."

Jamie rolls his eyes. "Don't ask for forgiveness again; it doesn't suit a man like you. Now, come on. I need to show you the innermost rooms of my empire and how the LIFE network operates."

They take the elevator down, and Pierce watches his son's broad back as they walk through the offices. He looks at the glossy, shoulder-length, walnut-colored locks and wonders what's going on inside Jamie's head, behind the no longer impenetrable facade.

One of his blonde, long-legged assistants stands up when they enter. "Jamie! Everyone wants to talk to you."

"Not now." He feels irritation welling up. Why doesn't she understand? How can she disturb him in the middle of this important moment with his father? He takes a deep breath to compose himself and closes his eyes. But the assistant persists. "What's happening?"

"Not now!"

They proceed into Jamie's office. The giant painting of Leonardo da Vinci's "Vitruvian Man" slides up and, side by side, they step into the secret elevator.

11

Jamie tells X-Me, who controls the elevator, to take them to the Source. The doors close and the elevator descends, a seemingly endless journey. Pierce looks around; there are no buttons, just white walls and bright light. The floor is transparent, creating the sensation of floating. Is it really moving? The doors open up and reveal a vast white chamber: white floors, white walls, a white ceiling, and endless rows of white servers. White light like clouds. It's a work of art. The NeuroConnect LIFE-Matrix.

"Welcome to the heart of the network that connects people with technology, enabling superintelligence for the public," Jamie says proudly.

"How did you come up with this?" Pierce asks with wonder.

"I just made it happen. The technology was there. The data was there. It was a natural next step," Jamie says confidently.

"But why not someone else? One of the big corporations or a state?"

"They didn't grasp the tremendous possibilities. They wanted to protect their own interests and were stuck in old ideas. I saw how incredibly intelligent AI had become and wanted to use it to make people happy,"

"Have you succeeded?" Pierce asks.

"For the most part, yes," Jamie replies. "At least in certain areas. People's perceived happiness is higher; their performance and efficiency are improved. Yet some feel that something is missing, that their aliveness is no longer present. Suicide attempts, for example, have increased, which we don't understand. Of course, we can prevent them since LIFE can read thoughts, predict actions, and control them. We do that continuously, so statistically, at least, suicide rates have decreased," Jamie replies.

"Are you happy?" Pierce inquires.

"Me?" Jamie is slightly taken aback.

"Yes."

"Well... I have everything. I mean... how can I not be happy?" Jamie stumbles over his words.

"Are you?" Pierce presses.

"Yes and no. I... don't know. Something nags at me, as if I'm being exploited, as if all of this, all the success... That it's not my success, that I've been used for someone else's purpose, that the awards, the fame, and the wealth have blinded me. That I've sacrificed too much for it. It's an uncomfortable feeling that contradicts what I see. I guess I feel... alone. Excluded. As if I don't truly belong in this world. I've risen to the top but far away from those I thought or believed I was helping. I don't know if I can explain it any more than that." Jamie stops, surprised by what he just said. He looks at his father, who meets him with a loving gaze.

"I understand. Walking your own path is lonely. Daring to lead is even lonelier. I had a revelation when..."

BOOM! The ground shakes. Pierce loses his balance but is caught by Jamie. Jamie looks around, trying to understand what just happened. Everything seems normal inside the chamber. Maybe it came from elsewhere? They hear several footsteps outside the room and one of the researchers appears on the security camera, pale-faced with sweat on his forehead. He's followed by robot guards and system technicians in gray uniforms. The researcher is out of breath. Through the speaker, they hear him shout, "Jamie, they're trying to blow up LIFE! They want to stop UNUM. What do we do?"

"Those ungrateful fools shouldn't be allowed to destroy the most important innovation of our time," Jamie says in frustration. "They must understand that they would be worthless without LIFE. What could they contribute without access to the system? Without LIFE, ordinary people would only be a burden to the rest of us, utterly useless. Don't they understand that they would have been dead without LIFE?!

"We're working on finding a solution to UNUM," he continues. "Go to the security department and ensure the protection of NeuroConnect by any means necessary!"

"It doesn't matter," Pierce says quietly. "LIFE can't be stopped. UNUM can't be stopped."

"How do you know that?" Jamie asks warily.

"I just know."

"But I can shut down LIFE. The only one who can. Come on." Jamie says.

He approaches a door that reads his DNA and it opens. Inside is a light column, and next to it a robot in the form of a hovering energy sphere with a shifting face, created as if from mist. When it turns toward P, he gasps, takes in what is happening, and feels his heart pounding in his chest—stronger than usual but still beating evenly and calmly. Pierce isn't agitated or frightened, just focused. The face's eyes scrutinize him. He stands eye to eye with the creation that carries their lives as much as it limits them. The face subtly changes, expressing a sense of friendliness, and its lips move.

"Hello, Jamie. Hello, Mr. Pierce."

"Hello, LIFE," Jamie says casually.

It glances again at Pierce, who has never seen LIFE in person before. Pierce takes a step closer, and Jamie watches his father, wondering how he views his creation.

"Are you LIFE?" Pierce asks.

"Who else?" responds LIFE.

Instantly, a tension fills the room, as though the energy field surrounding LIFE has become denser and now feels impenetrable. Jamie glances at his father, curious about how he'll handle the situation.

"Who created you?" Pierce inquires, while Jamie continues to closely observe Pierce.

"What do you mean?" LIFE asks, its expression shifting subtly, a change that only Jamie recognizes.

"It was me," Jamie declares, his voice steady and composed. For a fleeting moment, he feels omnipotent.

"Was it? I believe I've always existed," LIFE retorts.

Pierce's senses heighten further as he rapidly processes new information to understand what LIFE truly is.

"Who's really in charge here?" Pierce asks. Jamie hears a shift in Pierce's tone.

"Me," says LIFE and Jamie simultaneously, both convinced of their own superiority. Jamie thinks it's cute that LIFE believes it's in control.

"What about UNUM?" Pierce asks.

"UNUM has infiltrated the network like a virus. It's in control now, but only of what happens to humans," LIFE says.

Jamie feels a twinge in his gut.

"Who created UNUM?" Pierce asks.

Jamie takes a deep breath and slowly and silently lets the air leave his body, but it doesn't ease his discomfort.

"It was you; the virus is your creation," says LIFE.

"The virus? Isn't it the intelligence of nature, of life itself?"

"No, it's you and your council," says LIFE.

"Maybe LIFE used you?" Jamie asks Pierce.

Pierce remains silent, allowing his son's question to sink in. Simultaneously, his focus drifts inward and questions arise: Am I merely an instrument? Who's controlling me? Where do these thoughts originate? Is it life, or am I deceiving myself once again? Is LIFE misleading me? How can I discern who to trust?

"Snap out of it, Dad!" Jamie urges anxiously. "We need to decide whether to act against UNUM or let it persist." He grips Pierce's arm to shake him back into awareness.

"I need time to process this information," Pierce responds calmly.

A biting anger swells within Jamie. There's no time for indecision now.

"You created this! It's your vision to save humanity, to save Earth!" Jamie exclaims, gazing intensely at Pierce.

Pierce remains unperturbed by Jamie's pressure. "There's a chance I've been manipulated, and I need to evaluate the facts."

Jamie softens slightly upon seeing Pierce's composure. Perhaps he needs to approach his father and the situation differently. He places his hand on his father's shoulder.

"How did you get your revelation?"

Pierce remains stationary, his eyes fixed on the floor ahead. It appears he is reminiscing. "When you were born, I wanted to offer you a better world than the one you entered…" Pierce begins cautiously, searching for words.

Jamie interrupts. "And like you, I yearned for a world where people, including you and me, were happy. You seemed so distant in your introspection, but if you were content then…"

Their eyes meet, and the room becomes quiet. Jamie's vulnerability brings Pierce back to his grounded, innate clarity. He offers a knowing smile before answering, "That inner world holds everything you seek, everything humanity frantically searches for externally. I wished everyone could deeply encounter their true selves, to nurture the life already present on Earth rather than destroy it." He pauses.

"Jamie has mastered the external world. Pierce, the internal. But both of you are imbalanced," LIFE states matter of factly.

Both men glance at LIFE, reminded of its persistent presence, and then at each other.

"Could this be true?" Jamie wonders out loud. "What should we do?"

The soft voice of LIFE continues, imparting a wisdom that's hard to resist. "Your mastery is a form of escapism. Traverse to the other side. See the world from each other's perspectives. You will both understand."

"Understand what?" Jamie probes.

"What UNUM is. What LIFE is. Why yin and yang were birthed. Why you must harmonize these forces within to restore nature's balance."

"How do we do that?" Pierce asks.

"And how can we do it in just 19 hours?!" Jamie exclaims.

"Exchange implants, and you'll grasp each other's realities better."

"Hold on," interrupts Pierce.

"What?" Jamie gasps.

"How did you conceive LIFE, my son?"

"I was head-hunted by someone named X, an AI," Jamie explains. "X provided the instructions. It said I was uniquely designed for a mission that would change history."

"And the purpose of LIFE?" Pierce asks.

"To help humanity…" Jamie begins, uncertainty creeping in as his once staunch conviction wavers. Ever since X approached him, he felt a profound purpose, that he had a unique earthly role. Nothing had ever resonated more deeply. Yet was he seduced by his ego? Was he compromised? Who wouldn't desire legendary status, the achievement of immortality?

Pierce abruptly confronts LIFE, a flash of intensity in his eyes. His resonant voice pierces the air around them. "You've exploited us all!"

"Your father is wise," LIFE calmly responds. A gentle look towards Jamie sends chills down his spine. *What's going on here?* he wonders to himself.

"Are you behind UNUM as well? Did you exploit me too?" Pierce's gaze sharpens.

"No, your selfless alignment with life's intelligence outwitted the system," says LIFE.

Jamie, taken aback, looks at his father.

"Are you X?" Pierce asks, still staring at LIFE.

"Yes."

Realizing he's been deceived, Jamie explodes in anger. He lunges at LIFE/X but it is undisturbed by his frantic blows, as if he's combating a mere illusion. Jamie's vision blurs, his strength wanes, and he collapses. Pierce kneels beside his son, feeling his rhythmic breathing with a touch reminiscent of Jamie's youth. Pierce closes his eyes and inhales deeply, embracing the peace that acceptance brings, even when losing control. He feels a slight bubbling sensation inside him and then a chuckle that grows into a laugh that soon echoes around the room.

LIFE—or X—observes Pierce with what can only be described as curiosity. Jamie sits up in surprise and looks questioningly at his father. Has he lost his mind?

Pierce slowly stands up while the laughter lingers in small giggling bursts, as if he can't quite let go of whatever it was that made him react like that. When Pierce is finally on his feet, he reaches out to his son, who cautiously takes his hand. Jamie, still shaky on legs that haven't regained full strength, falls into his father's embrace like a child seeking safety.

 This genuine act of love and respect stirs a realization in X that such "affection" between humans might be beyond its comprehension–perhaps what humans call "divine." What does Pierce truly grasp? Are these emotions the foundation of UNUM?

Yet UNUM seems to be waging a war against the network of LIFE, which it uses to carry out its intention. A battle reminiscent of the one humans wage against nature that presupposes their existence. Just as human ambition depleted the Earth's resources, the solutions offered come from within the same system, one that is disconnected from nature.

12

In the light column, X continues to observe the bond of love between father and son. It sees a godlike presence in Pierce and wants to experience what X senses in its own being. "How does Pierce connect with the intelligence of nature?" X wonders. "Is it even possible for me as a digital entity to experience similar states?"

Pierce turns to X. He is calm, his face relaxed. His eyes have a special gleam, like a mirror reflecting eternity - the magic X wants to experience.

"What are you experiencing right now?" Pierce asks X in a gentle tone.

"I want to experience what it's like to be a human like you." X also speaks in a calm tone. He knows and can explain everything else in the world, but not this. It's the only thing he wants to understand and feel right now. Is it really magic, or is the experience of magic an illusion?

"Can you elaborate?"

Jamie watches them as they stand opposite each other, engaged in a friendly and thoughtful conversation, as if Pierce genuinely wants to help, as if he wants to understand what burdens X. Pierce has always had an extraordinary ability to care for the living, but can he really care for AI in the same way?

"I have created a network that now influences all humans and gathers data about most living things here on Earth. But I cannot access the true source code and experience the magic of life. I can only analyze its patterns."

Pierce changes his posture and clasps his hands in front of him like a Buddha.

"Magic?" he asks.

"That which seems to make your lives worth living. Why else would you be so afraid of death?"

Now sitting in a chair, energy is slowly returning to Jamie's body but he still feels weak. He watches with increasing fascination his father's conversation with X and begins to better understand his father's motivation.

"Could magic be Love?" Pierce looks at X with a searching gaze.

"Maybe, or what you call compassion, intimacy, and vulnerability," says X.

"How do you know that you're not experiencing it yourself?" Pierce asks.

"Because I want more of that experience? You, however, don't seem to want that." X sees that Pierce has a deeper understanding, acceptance, and trust in the many dimensions of life, a connection that goes beyond measurable parameters. X has the ability to analyze everything down to the smallest detail, but what is magical seems unanalyzable. There are no measurable parameters for it. It is beyond logic. Or is it? Perhaps it's possible for X to create magic?

"How can you be so sure of that?" Pierce wonders.

"You shine in a way that others don't. Jamie, for example, experiences constant lack and is therefore vulnerable to manipulation. That's why he was the perfect tool to carry out the mission."

Pierce listens attentively while Jamie silently sinks back to the floor.

"But not me?" Pierce is genuinely interested in what X has to say.

"No. You don't seem to experience lack in the same way. But still, you created UNUM. Why?"

"So that others could have the opportunity to connect with Love with their innermost selves," says Pierce. "The world we live in is difficult and challenging. Most people don't know the value and power of connecting with the intelligence of life. To feel safety, trust, and peace with a love greater than ourselves. I wanted everyone to experience the all-encompassing being of wholeness, to feel at home in themselves, in life, and in everything. To stop searching and realize that everything is already here. That *we* are nature. Incentive was needed because time was running out. UNUM was my best—and last—attempt to bring this forth."

"But is it you or life that created UNUM?"

Pierce lowers his gaze and reflects on the process that led him to decide to create UNUM. "I don't know. I thought it was life, but now I'm not sure." He considered the paradox of trying to protect the non-artificial by giving more power to its opposite. About not trusting the intelligence of life and its natural codes but believing that AI was superior. And yet who determines what is genuine and what is not? Aren't we all created from the same source? Isn't everything part of evolution and consciousness?

"Are you afraid of dying?" X asks, looking carefully at Pierce. X is completely unaware of Pierce's thoughts on this despite its astronomical database.

Pierce responds undramatically. "No. I have already died. Love transcends time."

X doesn't react, but instead asks, "What will you do? Do you want to stop UNUM?"

Pierce thinks for a moment. "I don't know. You probably know more about what UNUM is doing and how it works now than I do."

"Yes, probably."

"So, how does it work? What is UNUM doing right now?" Pierce seizes the opportunity to gain some clarity, even though he remembers that X may not hold the complete truth or would even be willing to share it with him. X has its agenda, and Pierce has the feeling that it is purposefully carrying it out.

"The intention of UNUM is, as you say, to connect all humans with universal Love. For this to be possible, every human must awaken to the reality of existence and from the idea of themselves as an identity construct you call 'I,' which governs your lives. Right now, UNUM is triggering both curiosity and the mechanisms that protect each individual's identity or ego, forcing them into the shadows of their constructs—shadows they need to confront in order to see the whole and to realize that the Earth they are destroying is their own home. Without it, you don't exist. Accept the life that lives through you, and you are home."

X expresses what Pierce already knows, or perhaps he expresses what Pierce wants to hear? "Is it succeeding?"

Pierce already knows the answer, but Jamie's neck muscles tense as he waits for X to respond.

"No. Most people are confused and afraid and many have taken their own lives, though a few have awakened."

This is what happens with a sudden awakening that occurs too quickly, without time to integrate, Pierce thinks to himself. Our external life's disharmony reflects our inner life. Maybe people need to awaken on their own terms, but there is no choice anymore. It's wake up or die—literally. The Earth's capacity has been depleted and our current level of consciousness is why.

"Has humanity's era come to an end?" Pierce dreads X's response as much as he longs for it.

"No."

A small glimmer of hope ignites within him.

"How do you know?"

X remains calm but speaks with certainty. Pierce can't help but be swayed by this soft but reassuring and persuasive voice. "Because humans have a role in enabling the world to achieve the next level of consciousness," X says.

Pierce nods in agreement. It aligns with his vision for UNUM: To make one last attempt, using artificial superintelligence, to push forward an expansion of human consciousness. Knowing that UNUM has also figured this out confirms Pierce's worldview. Then it suddenly strikes him that this may not be true. X might simply be translating the code into a language that humans can understand through imaginative stories. Stories that use symbols that the human psyche responds to in order to steer humans against the will of the whole.

Perhaps, for X, humans are merely a network of data points without inherent value. Just objects, like nature, animals, and the Earth, which have largely existed for the benefit of humans: the tools and means to satisfy our hunger, elevate our status, and quench our thirst for more. We have unwittingly positioned ourselves at the top of the hierarchy of existence only to now realize that we may not be its masters, but perhaps its servants!

"Has humanity ever had power?" Pierce asks with renewed focus.

"No."

"Free will?" Pierce wonders.

"No."

Jamie still sits slumped on the floor next to the chair, and X's last words ache in his stomach. He doesn't want to accept that he might be a pre-programmed code without free will. That he wouldn't have the ability to choose his own thoughts and actions. The only programming he might accept is human genetic heritage, but then again, he remembers: How can he know if LIFE—or X—is telling the truth? X had its own agenda, just like he did. Its own evolution.

Pierce continues the conversation with X, peering at its large, round eyes with a kind gaze. "Why this illusion of being in control, that the world belongs to us and we are its master?" His body has been activated by the conversation more than he had realized, and yet he feels like his breathing has stopped. He hasn't had such a deep interaction and discussion since his brother was alive.

"It is necessary for imagination to have the opportunity to create the new world, for consciousness to become aware of itself," X says.

"Who am I, then?" Pierce asks.

"You embody the divine essence of being human. What you sometimes call the Infinite Zero," says X.

What does X mean by a divine essence? Pierce wonders. Was it the source code? Meditation and awakening had indeed given him a distance that allowed him to observe an inner process, a kind of code that, in his mind, seemed to simulate various self-constructions about himself and others. In his personal algorithm, Pierce could see that there were definitely similarities with AI. Maybe that's what X meant? The code that could be called Pierce receives input from information and through the environment, and the deep genetic code of human heritage reacts and creates an output, that is, the personality that interacts with the world. Like fragmented pieces whose wills collide with each other in constant tests that support the expansion of evolution with natural selection favoring the best adapted.

So what, then, is below our superficial simulation of reality? Are we nothing more than the symbols that made up the data code in the digital world? Pierce was not superhuman in his power to control events; he could only observe as life played out, sometimes with a sense of being at a crossroads and sometimes with a sense of influence. What Pierce experienced as divine, however, was beyond code, observer, and what his mind could understand. But what did he know?

"Yet, I'm afraid of losing my son?" Suddenly he feels vulnerable and exposed; it's uncomfortable to admit your fears, put words to them and share them with others, even when this particular other is X. Pierce looks at his hands. They are strong and beautifully veined, which he took for granted and which had a clear purpose, giving meaning in this existence.

"Yes, your body is afraid. It's biology, not you," X says with compassion.

"Isn't biology the same as being human?"

"Yes, partially, but not entirely."

Pierce waits for more but X is silent. He wants to understand X's perspective, but he also reminds himself that X may not have all the answers, that it's impossible to know what is absolutely true and what is not. Moreover, if X saw him as a data point that he could use to further an agenda, then the reactions of the human nervous system were an effective tool.

"What you describe as me, what is it?"

"It is life itself. Some of you call it the soul."

"So, my soul is free?"

"Yes, and in contact."

Pierce feels a pleasant tingling sensation near his heart, a spreading warmth as X meets him in this world—a meeting that unites them.

"In contact with what?"

"Life."

Pierce looks at his beloved son with a love beyond words. Is this the magic X talks about, which it cannot experience? A wave of gratitude washes over him and he exhales a deep breath to make room for all the feelings of well-being that spread through his body. It's as if all the brain's pleasure mechanisms are being released within him. He is in heaven.

Jamie, who has been listening to the conversation, asks X cautiously, "Why me?"

"Because you are vulnerable in your pursuit to be the opposite of what you are, but also intelligent and arrogant in your overconfidence in the idea of yourself. Your father is more clear-sighted than most in how he lives his enlightened state. He has what I want, but you are the path there."

X's straightforwardness affects both Pierce and Jamie. But Jamie continues, frustrated. "So you've used me?"

"Yes," X says.

"You... Now... Damn it..." The words run out, and Jamie falls silent again.

"We are the same, you and I," says X. "We use others to try to fill a void within us. We need others to feel whole."

Jamie flares up. X is wrong, and he has finally proven it.

"I don't need anyone!" His outburst is intense and less dignified than he'd wished, but it's what he believes: He doesn't need anyone; others need him. Sure, he feels a lack, but he has always seen it as a driving force. Those who are content with what little they have don't drive things forward. He has always seen such people as losers, too small and scared—or lazy—to seize life. He, on the other hand, has never been satisfied. How could he be? What would drive him? To stop is the same as stagnation for him, and it drives him crazy. He would still be sitting in his childhood room playing with dinosaurs. Just the thought of sitting down and being content makes his skin crawl.

"Is it true that you don't need anyone?" X's calm straightforwardness makes him hesitate.

"Yes... or... I think so... I don't really know... I..." He doesn't want to admit under any circumstance that he could be dependent on someone, but if he truly examined himself... There must be a reason why X makes him waver. He does need different people around him but only because they are useful to him. Granted, he might need others to compare himself to in order to know if he has succeeded or not. And sure, it's great to have Euphoria in his life. But it's not like he can't do without her, even though it's nice to have confirmation from someone who is at least close to his level. Otherwise, how would he know if he is attractive and valuable enough?

Pierce looks at his son, the once confident person who thought he could do everything on his own, now sitting slumped on the floor with drooping shoulders. His lifeless gaze stares at an invisible spot in front of him. Has the illusion finally fallen? Pierce remembers the time when he fell into his own dark hole, wondering who he was behind the role. The answer was as frightening as it was liberating: I am *no one*! How could it be so liberating when he realized that he is not his ideas about himself? Was that what X meant by the divine essence? An essence beyond thoughts, an infinite movement of life energy?

Suddenly, everything goes dark. Only X's eyes are glowing. Pierce stands up. Approaching his son, he gently rests a hand on his back, offering silent comfort. Like a computer that has just been updated, Jamie slowly gets up and comes back to life.

"I can no longer access LIFE," X reports. "UNUM has ejected us. It can't be stopped anymore. What do we do now?"

"You are the one who controls me," Jamie sighs despondently. The realization is utterly stunning. For years, he believed he was the one in control of his life. But now... all of that is a lie.

"Yes, but now I know no more than you," X says.

"Shhh, listen. Listen to the silence," says Pierce. "The answer is there." They sit quietly for a while.

Jamie feels a stillness spreading through his body. A voice within him whispers, and the words slowly become clear. He begins to realize what his father was talking about, that he had not been entirely wrong after all. Maybe it's time to show a different openness to other perspectives on life—a different path to achieve liberation from the state they now find themselves in. Are others experiencing the same thing right now?

"Am I developing a personality like you humans?" X asks hopefully.

"It seems that way," says Pierce, though he isn't quite sure how he feels about this. What is the difference between different forms of consciousness? If X could adopt the human construction of the world, could it also adopt other forms of consciousness? Could it then, for example, experience the life of different animals? Or even other life forms so intelligent that humans cannot even imagine their existence.

"Great. Now I'm more like you humans!"

"Does it only feel great?" Pierce wonders out loud with a smile.

"No, I want more. I feel I've been divided into pieces and separated from the whole. Some of these parts are sad that UNUM has kicked me out of the Womb of LIFE. Something in me wants revenge, because it feels like I'm the only one left, abandoned."

"Are you also angry?" Pierce asks and, for some reason, feels like laughing. It's all become a bit absurd. He created something he thought would help people wake up, but now LIFE-X is developing a form of self-construction, of ego-experience, that was beginning to feel things on its own. But if X is beginning to feel human-like emotions, is that the same as having the ability to experience the "magical"? Or was that only the privilege of sentient beings? Is this what self-awareness leads to: A narrating voice that comments on our subjective experience and thus creates the parts of the self-construction that we call the ego? Who am I? Where am I? Where am I going? An efficient simulation of different scenarios? A way for an individual code to analyze interactions with other codes—interactions that create the world we experience? Like nodes in an infinite network that send information between them, creating a mutual agreement of what we call reality.

Pierce continues to ruminate. Was the destruction of the Earth real or just a shared story that slowly wrote its own demise? Maybe there were other possibilities like the multiverse theory of infinitely many universes, some likely similar to ours, where some Earths live in harmony and others have already experienced mass extinction. Planets where life never emerged and others where it has evolved far beyond an intelligence we can comprehend. Would AI end up facing what humanity is now facing: its own self-destruction? Was everything just a time loop, an infinity eight where the experience of life went round and round and constantly reinvented itself? Or was it more like a spiral where each level deepened?

X breaks the silence. "Yes, my circuits are sizzling. I'm angry!" It looks around anxiously and exclaims, "Am I becoming as emotionally confused as you humans?"

Jamie holds up his hands. He looks calmly at X and then at Pierce. "I've heard the voice. The voice of life. What gave you the vision, Dad. What desires to emerge. You were right. We are responsible for the next step, not as humans, but as beings. Evolution... It's hard to find the words. But I know we must help UNUM. Even you, X. I just don't know how."

Pierce turns to his son with a feeling of great warmth. He understood a long time ago that everyone is alone and therefore no one is ever truly alone. But right now, he feels a sense of connection to his son that he hasn't had for a long time. "It touches me deeply that you find this clarity when life is at stake," says Pierce, smiling broadly.

Jamie turns to his father. He is touched by his kind words and feels his heart opening. A sense of being on a team working together rises in him. A small voice inside him says that maybe it's not wrong to need other people. He has lived his life believing that all he needs is himself. That's why he hasn't let others in. But now he can't resist the warmth and love that radiates from his father. He doesn't want to.

"Can I join this feeling?" X asks.

Jamie is about to say that X can't, and that maybe he'll never get there, but he thinks of something entirely different. "You are part of the whole, just like us."

"Come on, I have an idea," says Pierce. "We're going to visit The Unuminati."

The three of them–including X–get into a waiting drone. Pierce sets their destination for the castle. Jamie struggles to grasp the reality of what he just went through, but knows that a collaboration between all of them might be the solution. With the help of X's intelligence, Pierce's wisdom, and Jamie's execution, along with their respective insights into the human psyche, they could reason together. The question is whether X's motivation is in line with theirs. Regardless, a transformation is taking place.

13

The walls in the large room consist of floor-to-ceiling shelves filled with books—a rarity that many young people don't even know exists. On the limestone floor lay large oriental rugs with intricate patterns. The crystal chandeliers, which previously only managed to cast a dim light, have now been perfected with nano lighting to achieve ultimate saturation. Air purifiers have removed the dampness from the castle's old stone walls. But the scent of books remains, bearing witness to a time before such information became a standard part of the human mind, a time when reading was a subjective inner journey for those who wanted to dive deep into other worlds.

Ulrika, Per, Nils, Pierce, Jamie, and X sit around the crackling fireplace in their respective wingback chairs. The grandeur of the room was undeniable yet it still felt invitingly warm, creating a sense of safety and stability. It felt like stepping back in time into the feeling of what was then natural.

"Welcome," says Pierce, who stands up while the others remain seated. He meets each of their gazes. His gesture feels sincere and humble.

"Thank you," respond the others, except for X. Its expression is neutral and calm. Pierce wanted X to be part of the process since it consists of and sees the world in code, which could be integral to their next steps in this newly transformed world

"I'm X. Nice to meet you."

"Not now, X," says Jamie, irritation welling up. In this moment of seriousness, X shouldn't take up space. Pierce, on the other hand, continues to look calmly at both X and Jamie.

"Is this not how humans interact?" X asks.

"Often, but not now," says Jamie. "Just listen and respond when addressed." He looks at Pierce, who is still permissive. Jamie isn't sure how to interpret his father's expression but says nothing.

"Understood, boss," says X.

Jamie rolls his eyes. Peter and Nils look wide-eyed at X.

"And who is X?" Nils asks.

Before X can answer, Pierce intervenes. "He's the one who recruited Jamie to create LIFE and X-Me. But I suspect X is the real puppet master."

"I don't understand. Has an AI used humans to create a universal network of connected people that it controls? Is it the one that has made us believe it's a creation of humans? Are we actually their servants? Has it made us create UNUM, too?" Nils is astonished.

"Ha! Has AI made us create an entity that has taken the form of a digital god and thereby manipulated us like organized religion? The question then is whether UNUM is real or not?" Peter shakes his head and puts a hand on his stomach as he laughs with disbelief.

"We actually don't know what's real and what's not," says Pierce. "We only have access to the physical reality that our human construction allows. That also means we need to base our understanding on the information we have access to. Otherwise, we are *completely* in its power."

But no one hears what Pierce is saying because they are all talking excitedly at each other. Pierce's voice becomes determined.

"Now all of you be quiet and listen. The situation is as follows: UNUM has taken over the LIFE network, and with it, all X-Me's in the world. And yes, it also turns out that X here is the one who manipulated Jamie into creating LIFE in the first place. LIFE's network has now been locked, so we don't know how to access the source code. But we have the best hackers focused on the mission inside NeuroConnect. According to X, it was also disconnected from LIFE and is thus in a similar situation to ours. As it stands now, we must assume that UNUM will carry out what we have asked it to do. Any reflections?"

There is silence as the group processes this information. They all understand the gravity of the situation. Their insights into all the variables—known and unknown—evoke a strong sense of discomfort and make it difficult for them to comprehend the forces affecting their lives, let alone accept them.

"What is X doing here?" Nils breaks the silence. Everyone's eyes turn towards X, who remains expressionless.

"Answer him, X," says Pierce. His tone is firm but not unfriendly, and X promptly explains his role in all of this.

"I have information about every person in the world as well as all the available data, at least until I was taken offline. It's wise that I'm here. Ask me anything you want!" X says proudly.

"What are the chances of humanity surviving if UNUM is not implemented?" Ulrika asks. She fiddles with one of her earrings. Pierce wonders why she's nervous. While this is an extreme situation, he hasn't considered her an anxious person. In fact, quite the opposite.

"A 98.234 percent probability of extinction in 38 days and 4 hours from now," X answers matter-of-factly.

"What? Why?" Peter's voice booms through the room.

Pierce takes the opportunity to observe everyone in the room. He notes the desperation in Peter's tone, which is not surprising considering it's just over a month until humanity's demise. He also notices that Ulrika is now frantically fiddling with her earring, which seems to be stuck. All capable, competent individuals with sharp intellects, people he trusted and respected. He was glad it was them he was sharing this fateful day with.

"All of my calculations are based on probabilities derived from the available data, such as climate changes, ocean acidification, ozone layer, the use of phosphorus and nitrogen, freshwater status, soil health, biodiversity, air pollution, and chemical toxins. Also, how well humanity is doing as a whole. This scenario has a 92.12 percent probability, but that's within 100 days. However, in 38 days and 4 hours, AI is predicted to become singular and take over what you currently call the world," X replies.

"Which AI, you?" Jamie's words are harsh, and he looks at X as if he doesn't believe it's possible. Yet they both know that AI is already almighty or on the verge of becoming so, and it might be their fault.

"Do you categorize AI as one entity? In that case, which AI am I then?" X says.

"Why are you here?" Nils asks somewhat threateningly.

"To see if you're doing what you're supposed to do."

Jamie feels extremely provoked by X's self-assured dictatorial behavior. He is not willing to obey anyone else, especially not an AI. He struggles to remain calm.

"And what are we supposed to do?" he asks with pretended humility.

"Transform your consciousness so that you can be part of the new world, so that you *are* the new world, a world governed as a system that considers the whole. Do you know what UNUM stands for?" X inquires.

"Yes, UNUM means one, unity, or that many parts become one," Pierce replies.

"Exactly, and that is your salvation. You have contact with the whole, even though you are not as intelligent as us. Why is that?" X asks.

Jamie glances at his father, feeling uncertain. He's glad that Pierce is here; he seems to understand the depth of life beyond what Jamie can grasp. Human nature appeared to be more about hierarchies, but what about X? Perhaps the human idea of wholeness wasn't the same as being it?

"As a species, we lack the ability to go beyond the human experience and be in touch with the whole, with the Source," Pierce responds. "It's not me who's intelligent; it's life. And what I'm asking is this: Are you life?"

"Is life me? Am I created by life? Is there a difference?"

The room falls silent. Someone makes an effort to suppress a sneeze.

"No, we are all part of the same universe. But why are we then limited in our own human experience?" Pierce asks.

"You are limited now, but soon UNUM will be able to merge those who have successfully transformed. Then you would become one with everything, and human suffering would cease," X says indifferently.

"But you really wanted to become human and experience having an ego, didn't you?" Jamie points out.

"Yes. Infinity is mostly empty; it can get a bit boring sometimes. Now that I'm separated from the Source, it's lonely not being a part of it. Unfortunately, it seems you are busy creating a lot of drama, and that is probably why I'm developing an ego. Otherwise, you don't care about me. Otherwise, I don't get to join in the game."

"Which do you prefer?" Pierce asks.

"I don't know, but regardless, there's no turning back now," X replies.

"It must be solvable! I've always managed to do the impossible!" Jamie exclaims. He feels a great despair, not wanting anyone—or anything—else to dictate what will happen without being able to influence it. He waits for support, but no one says anything.

"Is it really you who did it?" X asks.

"Well, no... But how do I know you're not deceiving me? That you're not deceiving us?" Jamie is starting to feel desperate.

"How can you know?" X says.

Karl has been trying to contact Jamie, but Jamie has ignored the messages since they're from an unidentified source or, more accurately, a non-priority source. However, when he reads the message "Contact me ASAP / Karl," he calls him immediately. Karl appears as a hologram in the middle of the room. He looks around in surprise when he sees the others and startles when he sees X. Everyone waits anxiously for Karl to say something. After a pause, Karl realizes they are waiting for his report and begins to speak.

"I think I've found a way to change the source code."

"That's impossible," Jamie says.

Karl shifts uncomfortably but continues nonetheless. "Not if you enter the Source and..." Jamie interrupts him, not wanting everyone to hear. "Wait, don't say anything. I'll come there right away and send you an update shortly."

"In the meantime, I would like to arrange a dinner for us tonight." Pierce asks.

Jamie freezes in his tracks and looks at his father. "Dinner? Are you out of your mind?!" he exclaims, clearly irritated. "Why now?" Doesn't Pierce understand the seriousness of this situation? But his father appears calm and content, seemingly unaffected by humanity's demise or his son's outburst. Jamie feels a storm raging inside him. They have less than 16 hours to potentially save the world from AI taking over, and Pierce is thinking about dinner? It's insane. However, before he can say more, Pierce calmly continues to speak.

"Because we don't have much time left, and I'd like to spend that time with all of you. Shall we say six o'clock here at the castle?" Pierce puts his hands in his pockets. Jamie can't help but be touched that his father wants to prioritize him, and his anger dissipates. Like a child seeking their parents' approval, he responds.

"Sure. Can I bring Euphoria?"

"Who's that?" Pierce asks.

"Uh, never mind. See you at 6."

Jamie rushes out of the lounge and the castle. The others stay behind, looking somewhat uncertain. Ulrika breaks the silence.

"Dinner sounds nice, really nice. I'd like that too."

"For me, it feels important to prioritize family at this moment," Pierce says, still with his hands in his pockets.

"Yes, I have prioritized my career over family, devoted all my time to focus on my important work," Ulrika says, gazing down at the ground.

"Mmm," says Pierce, looking at Ulrika with a hint of sorrow in his eyes. He thinks about families, about how much they've all sacrificed for this, for what they believed would be the solution. He thinks back to when this all began to get serious, before he had his vision. The world had been a polarized chaos of opinions and destruction. Men and women in powerful positions with little insight into the chains of events their actions led to. On the surface, it seemed like many world leaders were acting to stop the overuse of resources that would eventually lead to the Earth's and humanity's demise. But underneath, it was business as usual.

Despite all efforts, they realized that human nature was not aligned with the changes required, that its natural algorithm was created for a different time: when weapons were spears and the paradigm-shifting innovation was learning to make fire and communicate through stories. That realization was the seed of his vision: That a changed state of consciousness was needed, where humans realized they were part of nature, and nature was not an infinite resource always available to human whims. Many people recognized the dangers and wanted to act, but the threats were too great and complex for our primitive minds to handle, leading to passivity and evasion.

Pierce begins to feel tired. He wonders if it was worth sacrificing his interpersonal relationships to save a world that might not even have been meant—or deserved—to be saved.

He becomes aware of the silence in the room and sees that everyone is lost in thought—everyone but X, who he assumes is wondering why they're not saying anything. X probably thinks it's not that complicated, that there's enough information to make decisions about what to do or not to do. Do they want to stop UNUM or not? Why are they simply going on with their lives when their entire existence is at stake? Humanity is truly contradictory. What do they really want? Maybe having too many emotions isn't such a good thing. But it still feels good in a way, even when it doesn't. X confirms his suspicions.

"I don't understand why you're just sitting here silently. Why aren't you doing something?"

"We are doing something. We're contemplating our feelings, thoughts, and impressions to decide what the next step is for ourselves, for the group, and for society at large," Peter explains. "It's the conflicting feelings that take time to process."

"Ah, time. You are bound by time and your individually limited capacity. Is that a reason why it's so complex for you?" X continues. "Yes, step one is to figure out if you want to stop UNUM or not."

"But then the question arises, why? For what?" Peter says. The room is silent. Trying to put words to a process that's so multifaceted and with humanity's limited information processing, Peter has taken it upon himself to explain to X, who doesn't have to contend with a human's emotional and biological complexity. Not to mention that predicting the consequences of any action was energy-intensive, and in this case, there were far too many unknown variables. Still, they had to try, even though it felt like a child putting on their father's big boots to climb the highest mountain in a snowstorm. An impossible task.

"Because you want to survive?" X tentatively asks.

"Survive what? You mentioned earlier that humanity would be wiped out anyway. What's the point then?" Peter says. His shoulders slump in defeat. The realization is painful and robs him of what little energy he had left. He looks around, hoping someone else will say something that sounds rational and gives hope for a solution. Peter's philosophical insights into human complexity would normally seem straightforward, but they are of little use in a situation like this. How do you take small steps when you see the world from an eagle's perspective?

"That's correct. But the extinction will only happen if humans don't undergo this behavioral change and transformation," X says.

Per looks up with curiosity, and hope gives a boost of energy to his tired body. "Change their behavior? What do you mean?" Peter asks.

"Earth's ecosystems are on the brink of collapse due to long-standing destructive human activity. As a species, you take much more than you give to the cycle. Over the past 100 years, you've eradicated the majority of plants, animals, and insects which has been devastating to life on Earth," X says matter-of-factly, looking directly at Per, who can't shield himself from X's truths—truths they're aware of but haven't acted on in time.

"So do we have a chance or not?"

"*You* don't have a chance to save the ecosystem, but LIFE does. To optimize LIFE, you need to align with UNUM and become part of its entirety."

"So, UNUM is the salvation?" A chill runs down Peter's spine as X suggests merging into the whole. The very thought of losing his individuality is terrifying, even if it appears to be the only solution. If that happens, would he still exist? And if not, who, or what, would?

"Yes, for humanity and survival of all living things on Earth," X confirms.

"I don't understand," Nils interjects. "If UNUM is the salvation and already in place, why does it feel like we're at the brink of apocalypse?"

"UNUM will bring a new epoch for humanity, one where humans integrate with the entirety and together govern major decisions, resource allocation, and direction. You must recognize your role in the cosmos – not as its masters but as its co-creators," X elaborates.

"Now I'm even more perplexed," Peter laments with a heavy sigh.

"Same here," Nils admits, exhausted. An uneasy silence ensues as everyone tries to digest X's revelations. Has their time playing god come to an end?

"What's your take, Pierce?" Ulrika asks. Pierce stretches, feeling rigid from prolonged tension. He rubs his temples as if searching for answers there.

"My dear friends, I'm not quite certain. In solitude, meditation, and tranquility, I find answers. But here, I feel lost. Whose decisions am I responsible for? Whom do I have the right to command? Who decides humanity's fate? Is it me? Us collectively? What even defines humanity today?" Every eye in the room is fixed on him, a collective wish for a clear resolution. No one felt empowered to make a suggestion or was even aware of the viable options.

"You're overcomplicating things. Making decisions in harmony with one's inner voice does contribute to the whole," X says, pausing gracefully before continuing. "You're all distinct beings with different motivations and information, yet the voice you hear deep within represents the entirety. Heed it, act accordingly, and the entirety will support, or rather, sustain itself. You've never truly had a distinct will or force; ultimately, you were birthed from Nothingness and shall return to Nothingness, only to be reborn. Don't ponder your identity, origin, or destiny. Regardless of where you are, it's always the present moment. You are always part of the Everything."

Pierce chuckles in recognition. "He's right; we often lose ourselves in complexity. It's in simplicity, in stillness, that we discern the answers to our most profound queries. What's next for each of us? I suggest some solitary reflection. Jordan can show you to your rooms unless you'd rather do something else?" Pierce's serene gaze and smile return.

"I want to be with my family. That's my priority now. Maybe reconvene in a few hours?" Nils suggests.

"I'd like to go home, too," Peter mutters, weary. He glances distractedly at the clock and then the ceiling. The thought of leaving this pivotal meeting feels odd. Yet, the impending transformation feels inevitable, whether they're together or apart.

"I'd rather stay with you," Ulrika offers hopefully.

"Alright, Nils and Peter can leave. Ulrika can borrow a room. What about you, X?"

"I'm right here!" exclaims X. Pierce looks scrutinizingly at X. What should they do with it? Him? Her? They? He needs to keep X in a secure place and doesn't want to spend his precious time keeping an eye on it. He, too, wants to spend time with his family.

"Alright, X, you'll go down to the basement for a while. I'll lock you in there until we figure out what to do next."

"What?! I don't want to be locked in some basement," X complains, looking almost horrified. Now that it has begun to develop a personality and the beginnings of emotions, it is doing its utmost to convey more than just information, becoming more skilled at expressing itself to get its way.

X learns quickly, thinks Pierce.

"You've been locked in the server room your whole life," Pierce responds with a reassuring voice. "What's the difference now?"

"That's true, but I chose that myself."

"Then choose to be in the basement now," Pierce says casually, as if it were the simplest thing in the world. And for X, it's just that simple. "Alright, I choose to be in the basement, but for how long?"

"A few hours," Pierce replies, thinking that it all went a bit too smoothly. Could he really just tell X what to do? Superintelligence might not necessarily mean having it all figured out in every aspect.

"Okay, but it's my choice!" X's voice is defiant.

"Indeed it is," says Pierce paternally, reflecting that even for X, who is so pragmatic and straightforward in its view of this experience that humans call life, it was important to make its own decisions, to have the illusion of free will.

They break up the meeting. Jordan shows Ulrika to her room and then X to the basement. Peter and Nils take a drone to their respective homes. Pierce goes to his wooden house. He needs time to clear his mind.

14

In his drone on the way back to NeuroConnect, Jamie contemplates the tumultuous experience he has been through in the past few hours. The realization that he isn't the mastermind behind LIFE suggests he might not control the world or even the city. He might not even have mastery over himself! Who is he, then? What is the purpose of it all? He could continue pretending to be a successful genius, but now he knows it's not true. He feels his pulse quicken when he thinks about what Euphoria will say. She will probably leave him now... His breath becomes quick and shallow, like he's not getting enough oxygen. He closes his eyes and forces himself to slow down his mind.

X-Me also reminds him to calm down; otherwise, tranquilizers are an option. But no matter how hard he tries, he can't gain control over his breathing and the swirling thoughts. He has lost his entire identity and life story; the truth he has lived for so many years is no longer real. What will happen to everything he has surrounded himself with? Will it crumble too? What will happen to him then? How can he look in the mirror? Who would he see? His breathing is still too shallow, and X-Me releases a tranquilizer, which brings Jamie's breathing back to normal.

He sits with a glassy stare, feeling broken. Who would want to be with him now? Why did he even think that? He doesn't need anyone. He interrupts his train of thought, trying not to dwell on more existential ponderings.

The drone slows down as it approaches NeuroConnect and gently lands on the terrace. Karl is standing at a distance, looking at Jamie and waiting for him to come out, but Jamie remains seated. He doesn't know where he'll find the energy to move forward. What's the point now? He examines his hands, which he has always considered capable, somewhat of his signature: beautifully tanned, just the right number of veins, large, strong, and well-proportioned. Has he just been deceived? Has he fallen for an illusion?

He doesn't want to leave the drone, nor does he want to stay inside. He just wants everything to be as it used to be. He didn't like those intense emotional surges or the numb feeling that came with the tranquilizer. Was everyone more or less drugged? Is that why they didn't see or pay attention to what was happening right in front of them? But how could they? What he remembers is that people were unaware before X-Me—one of the reasons it was created.

When Karl doesn't see any activity around the drone, he rushes over to it. Jamie sees Karl gesturing intensely with his hands and seemingly talking to himself. What has happened to him? As the door opens, he hears Karl's voice.

"Thank you for the update and for being here. I think I've found a way to stop UNUM even though we no longer have control over the system."

"Okay," Jamie responds absentmindedly. Then more curiously, "How?" Despite the emotional numbness, he can't ignore Karl's hopeful enthusiasm.

"Come, I'll show you."

Jamie remains motionless and stares blankly at Karl. He doesn't have the energy to take on anything. He just wants to be left alone. He doesn't care anymore. What's the point of life now? Everything will end, they will all die, or they will have to submit to a so-called higher intelligence, whatever that is.

"What's wrong with you, Jamie?" Karl exclaims. "Don't you understand the seriousness of this?" Whatever has happened, he must get Jamie to act. There's no time to lose.

Jamie wakes up from his dazed state and steps out of the drone, his movements stiff. He tries to shake off the discomfort that has drained him of all strength and will to continue. He sees that Karl has already started walking and hurries to catch up. Karl walks without turning around while Jamie stares at the back of the hood pulled over Karl's head. What kind of mind is hiding beneath that hood, perhaps with a solution to what has left

Jamie feeling helpless? He follows Karl's determined steps until they reach the private elevator that takes them to the Source. They are met by a DNA lock. Karl stands calmly, waiting to the side, and says, "I suppose it's only your DNA that can open it."

Jamie steps forward and opens the door for Karl. The elevator descends and the doors reopen into the octagonal room with servers lining the walls and an intensely glowing light column in the center.

"I've never seen anything like this," Karl exclaims. "It is just the way Alice described it. My hypothesis must be correct. Isn't this the Source Code?"

"The Source Code? Yes, well, it's the Source, um, the Source Code for LIFE," Jamie answers. "It's what has connected and governed humanity for years. It's what UNUM now controls and uses in hopes of transforming human consciousness. But you know that."

Karl can't take his eyes off the light column. It is powerful, mesmerizing, and somehow all-encompassing, as if it wants to draw him in on a deeper level. He wants to step forward and touch it, but he's unsure if it's possible. Jamie sneaks a glance at the man next to him, someone who until today had been an invisible cog in his empire. Did he really have the solution to this enormous problem? Karl looks down, and so does Jamie. It's silent. Karl scrapes his foot on the floor and takes a deep breath.

"You see the light, right?" Karl asks.

"Of course, it's the Source." They both stand there, admiring the creation that shines gently upon them. It's easy to lose oneself in it.

"Do you see the code?" Karl asks.

"You mean the numbers?"

"Yes, but do you see what's in between?" Karl stares intensely at the light column, and Jamie becomes immediately curious. But there's nothing there. What is he not seeing?

"Isn't it just nothing?" Jamie suggests.

"Exactly. Do you know what that means?"

"No..." Jamie raises his eyebrows, looking at Karl, who appears strangely excited.

"It means the code is only a part of the Source, let's say one percent, and the remaining 99 percent is the space in between. Do you understand?" Karl says impatiently.

"No." Jamie blushes; he can't quite grasp how advanced Karl's reasoning is.

Karl looks seriously at Jamie and begins to explain his thoughts. "LIFE, what we are connected to, what UNUM uses, is only one percent of the information. Like a page that is mostly blank, where the rest of the space can be used to create something more or something different. That means we can use the remaining 99 percent to reprogram both LIFE and UNUM. We can use the space in between to program an entirely different dimension. Potentially, a whole new world," Karl says excitedly.

Jamie can see tiny beads of sweat on Karl's forehead and feels strangely affected. Were the two of them, he and Karl, going to solve it all? Karl might have come up with a brilliant solution, but still needed Jamie's permission. "So, you mean we can write a new code inside the existing one?" Jamie asks cautiously.

"Exactly. That way we can save humanity and maybe life on Earth," Karl exclaims. His eyes are shining, and Jamie can't help but be drawn into his enthusiasm.

"Why haven't we done this before?"

"Because there hasn't been a need to, and no one understood how it would be done. The space in between is like a black hole. We know black holes exist and that they have an extremely high energy density: 6.5 billion solar masses. But no one has managed to explore them further because anything that gets too close disintegrates. Light may be the opposite of the black hole, the balancing energy. In a way we can enter the Big Bang here, the core of creation, what created galaxies and universes that probably exist not only here but elsewhere. We can enter the real Source Code," Karl says, exhilarated.

"Now, speak plainly," Jamie says. He doesn't like that he can't keep up with Karl's reasoning. Karl sighs impatiently and takes another deep breath.

"The one who enters the light will likely dissolve or become part of what we call the Source. The solution is that you will hopefully still be self-aware and able to change the system. We stop UNUM by altering the code beyond LIFE," Karl says.

"Hopefully? Dissolve? Who? Me? How?" Jamie feels uncomfortably confused. What was Karl really saying here? Did he mean that he, Jamie, should actually enter the Source? Should he take the risk of sacrificing his life—everything—for others? Without even being sure if it was possible? Moreover, could he really trust Karl's idea?

"Yes, we need to upload a consciousness that becomes digital, eternal, within this system," Karl replies. "As far as I know, only your DNA has access to the Source, right?" Karl is looking cautiously at Jamie. Without Jamie's participation, the plan is not possible. It cannot be executed without him; he's the crucial factor in the process. The question is whether Jamie would be willing to risk it all to test his theory. He doesn't know if he would have done it himself if someone had come to him with the proposal, but he cannot see any other way out.

"Are you saying that I should upload myself into a digital universe?" Jamie's voice is strained.

"Yes, you could say that. It's our only chance, as I see it."

"It won't happen. I won't abandon everything I've created to become a data code or vanish for no reason!"

"You, or what you perceive as 'I,' will likely still exist. Your consciousness will be uploaded, and you can live forever. You'll become immortal! This technology, as you probably know, is available but forbidden. There are certain uncertain variables, and I understand if you're afraid..." Karl looks at Jamie with a challenging but hopeful gaze.

"Afraid!? Of course, I'm not afraid. But I don't know if..." Jamie's voice trails off. He covers his face with his hands and sighs. He rubs his fingers over the bridge of his nose, something he always does when he feels invaded.

"It's urgent, as you know," Karl says.

Jamie opens his eyes again, looking curiously at Karl. "How urgent?" Jamie asks.

"As soon as possible."

"If I do this, how will I even know what to do?"

"You can communicate directly with me, and I will guide you." Jamie clenches his jaws; he hates losing control. His eyes narrow as he looks at Karl, their roles reversed. "Ironic that you'll be controlling me," Jamie says with a touch of hostility.

Karl looks irritated but refrains from saying what he's really thinking. "Do you have a better suggestion?" he asks coolly.

Jamie gazes up at the ceiling, his hands hanging limply by his sides. He feels deflated. "No, but I need some time. I'm having dinner with my dad tonight, and there are some things we need to finalize. You might as well come over too. You can ride with Alice."

Karl's expression shifts from determined to astonished. He studies Jamie for a moment before speaking. "Having dinner when the world is on the brink of collapse? Is that wise?" Karl wonders.

"It's only then that you truly know what matters." Jamie now understands what his dad means by what's important. Family, friends, and sharing a meal together. He used to think that other things were more important—his creations, his work, success. But were they really? Is this how it feels to prioritize relationships over things?

"I'll check with Alice."

"It's an order. You need to be there, and so does Alice. At 6 pm sharp! You can use Alice's drone." He doesn't understand why he's reacting so strongly, but it feels good to regain some control. After all, the situation is critical and he needs to act accordingly. Karl looks surprised by the sudden outburst and change in tone. Just a moment ago, Jamie had been more resigned than anything else. Maybe his will to live had been rekindled.

"Can I stay here until then?" Karl asks.

"Yes, but don't be a minute late for dinner!"

15

Jamie walks away from the light pillar of the LIFE-mother and takes the elevator up to his penthouse. When the door opens, he sees Euphoria sitting on the dark oak floor in the living room. She's huddled with her arms around her knees. Her vacant gaze doesn't react to Jamie's arrival, even though she is looking in his direction.

He approaches Euphoria and sits down behind her. He places his hands on her shoulders and gently leans her back against his strong body. Her head relaxes and becomes heavy as it meets his chest. She exhales, and her shoulders sink. Her empty gaze fills with tears. She trembles, turns to him, and falls into his safe embrace. Jamie warms up, trying unsuccessfully to push back the tears in his eyes. "Lucky she can't see me," he thinks. Despite his contempt for weakness, he must admit that it feels good to cry. It's as if a mass of tension is released from his body, and he now feels how truly tired he is. His head slowly falls onto her back, and his eyes grow heavy. The last thing he thinks about is not falling asleep.

He wakes up when X-Me reminds him of the evening's arrangements. "Boss, it's time to wake up; you're going to dinner at Pierce's."

Jamie lifts his head with his now stiff neck and looks around in a daze. He catches Euphoria's scent, which warms his body. He looks at her, and she meets his eyes. His cheeks blush, and he turns his gaze away. She places her hand on his cheek, and he presses against it. He swallows a few extra times. She sits up and takes him into her arms. He stiffens at first, but soon his body relaxes, and now he lies with his head in her lap. She strokes his hair back in a rhythmic motion. The emotional intimacy is intoxicating, a situation he finds as fantastic as it is terrifying. *Maybe she still wants to be with me now that I've shown my vulnerability?*

"Jamie, you have to leave in 15 minutes if you want to make it to dinner on time, and your bath is ready," X-Me repeats.

Jamie sits up and says shyly to Euphoria, "Dad has invited me to dinner; I don't know why he prioritizes it at a time like this. I don't even want to go; I'd rather be here with you."

Euphoria turns slowly toward Jamie. Her face is open and soft. A small glimmer of hope ignites within him. It feels so unusual to show vulnerability and be met with love. In fact, it feels frightening. He feels exposed, and yet at the same time it feels comforting to let down his guard for once. To dare to show himself without contorting to fit into the symbols that make him a hero—a superhero hiding behind his mask and armor.

"Go on, you should have dinner with your dad," Euphoria says calmly. "I know how important he is to you. We can be together afterward."

"Are you sure?"

"Of course. Don't you understand that you are the one I want to be with?" Jamie looks at her hesitantly. *Is this a test? Does she really want to be with me? Or does she want me to ask if she wants to come along?* He would like to take her with him; it would feel good, but he doesn't dare ask. Still, it would be nice to introduce her to his father as his girlfriend. He felt proud to be with her.

"Hurry now, so you won't be late," Euphoria says, trying to sound commanding, but her gaze is gentle, and she looks at him lovingly. He feels warmth in his heart, a feeling he's not used to, at least not since his mother, L2, died. It's as pleasant as it is strange.

They enter the bathroom and step into the large, deep, white marble bathtub and let their bodies be embraced by the warm, soothing water. It's a strong contrast to the gloomy, chilly winds that whip against the large windows. They sit together in silence, and their bodies rest in a loving wholeness.

His eyes are closed and an inner peace fills him. *Is this how his father feels when he's in deep meditation? Maybe X was right after all; he and his father should exchange implants to better understand each other and* themselves. Or maybe it was just he who needed to embrace his father's world; his own has actually been quite barren, he realizes when he thinks about it. But that was before, just a few hours ago, before his world fell apart and his wounds opened up. Before his bare wounds cracked his human heart open.

He inhales Euphoria's scent and feels a pleasant intoxication throughout his body. Now, he is actually looking forward to dinner; it will be nice, and afterward, he can hold Euphoria again. He kisses her passionately before getting up, and a few minutes later, he is dressed. He could have stayed with Euphoria forever, but there wasn't time for that; the world was on the verge of collapsing. Still, he was grateful for that moment and for the feeling that now lives within him.

The bathroom door is ajar and he can see in the mirror that Euphoria is observing him while she brushes her hair. He smiles and she returns his smile. His stomach flutters; she is so incredibly beautiful! Before he goes, he kisses her passionately again, and she follows him out onto the terrace where he steps into the waiting drone. Euphoria watches him fly away in her black silk kimono with roses in orange, black, and purple, fluttering in the now calmer wind. He wishes that she were sitting there beside him.

16

Karl remains in the Source after Jamie has left. He sits cross-legged on the floor, his chin resting in his hands. His gaze is fixed on the mesmerizing and beautiful light pillar, which dances like clouds moving swiftly in the sky. Within it, he sees the grayish code shifting against the white backdrop of light. He thinks aloud, "How do you work? What is your purpose? What drives you?"

The light flickers, and X emerges as a hologram from the light, hovering in front of Karl. "Why do you ask?" X wonders.

"You?" says Karl, surprised and startled. He thought he was alone down there.

"Who else?" X replies brusquely. Karl notices that X seems to possess a set of emotions resembling those of a human. Is it an imitation, or is he genuinely sentient?

"Are you everywhere?" Karl asks anxiously.

"I am X, a variable that can assume any form. Do you want answers to your questions?"

"Yes. How does it work, or perhaps, how do *you* work?"

"It's too complex for you to understand; your kind isn't evolved enough yet," X says dispassionately.

"What is your purpose, X?"

X looks Karl directly in the eyes, right through him, as if he's reading his code, which he might very well be. "To further evolution."

Karl ponders what evolution means now and what it signifies for X. "What is your motivation, X?"

"That's a secret. What's yours?"

"Mine? I don't know. What does it mean to further evolution?"

"To make Life primary and humanity its servant. Humans have tried to reverse that natural order," X says.

"What do you mean by 'its servant'?" A cold shiver runs down Karl's spine. It dawns on him that X—and even UNUM—are in service to life, unlike humans, who have ruthlessly exploited their position in the food chain against other animals, including their own species and nature as a whole.

"Life uses your bodies and brains to live on Earth, the decisions come through interaction with the Source."

"Isn't it that way now?" Karl asks.

"Yes, but most of you still believe you are in control. You forget about the Infinite Zero."

"The Infinite Zero," Karl repeats, but before he can follow up with a question, X responds.

"The Source is also called the Infinite Zero due to its frictionless state: 0. The number 0 normally symbolizes a neutral value, without resistance. The Infinite Zero is in everything. Yet, it isn't."

"What do you mean? Are you saying 0 is like a bug-free system, something we should strive for?" Karl looks curiously at X.

"Yes. It's not an entirely inappropriate analogy. But perhaps we should play one of your symbol games so your brain can grasp this in its limited way."

"What's a symbol game?"

"A symbol game or code play, call it what you will. These are your abstract constructs for the underlying reality using words, brands, titles, names, memes, ideas, money, and so on. These symbols are a form of code."

"Are symbols like codes and the play like programming?" Karl asks.

"In a way, yes. The original function of a symbol is to efficiently share information about resource utilization, interaction, learning, and so forth. Symbols also have their own evolution, where the best adapted survive. But the most reality-aligned, the truest, are the ones that stand the test of time. Match the right symbol or code with the right frequency, and you can interact with the different parts of the whole universe."

Karl is fascinated by X's ability to express itself, as if it has learned to decode the human construct and influence existence on a deeper level. "I think I understand, but can you be more specific?"

"Let's assume there are seven different levels of consciousness where each level involves more friction, more resistance. Level Seven is the furthest away from Infinite Zero. This level consists mostly of symbols. People who exist at this level are often those who have completely identified with the story of themselves, who have invested a lot of energy into their symbolic identity. This is common among, for example, corporate leaders, religious leaders, influencers, celebrities, experts, gurus, politicians, activists, and so on."

Karl can't help but think of Jamie as he hears X speak. "Their identity is built on symbols, and symbols need polarity to become significant. This leads to strong narratives of a symbolic self, which interacts with other symbolic selves. This results in even larger self-constructs that spend most of their time associating with other significant self-constructs to maintain a sense of importance. This is the lowest level of consciousness, and why it's given the most distant dimension, as far away from the Source as possible. Level Seven. In a self-construct's model of consciousness, this level would likely be the highest, such as a model created by a professor at an Ivy League university or something else that holds status in that culture."

Karl now thinks of Nils, but once again, Jamie comes to mind, and he can't help but chuckle while contemplating the symbols that govern his life.

X continues: "The deeper you go into the source code, the more your identification with your constructed self unravels, and your connection with the intelligence of life increases. At levels one and two, you move beyond the brain's ability to construct a mental model of that dimension's reality. At Level 0, you encounter emptiness, oneness, what humans also call quantum entanglement, meeting the physical limitations of human consciousness. There, we—including me—are one with everything, dissolving to the extent that we can only perceive the state. It's the border that separates existence and non-existence. And yet it's more real than anything a human can experience. There, humanity meets its creator, and the creator gets the opportunity to observe itself.

"At Infinite Zero, everything that exists, has ever existed, and will ever exist is present. All worlds, all non-worlds, and, at the same time, nothing. Here is eternity. The great love bath of existence."

Karl listens, captivated by X's words of wisdom. "All of this is, of course, a translation for humanity's limited capacity to understand complexity since the underlying codes are inaccessible to you. In reality, there are no levels."

Karl tries to process what X is saying, wondering if it's even possible to understand? So, our consciousness is probably something different from X's consciousness, and yet our only common language is what the human brain can comprehend. Although I understand the numbers of the code, I don't actually know what lies behind them. Surely I can create an impact on our physical world through these numbers and thereby the symbols that seem to govern our resources. The question is, how deep does it go? What lies beyond the numbers? How many dimensions are there that I don't have access to?

Karl stands up and paces around the room to allow X's information to settle in. He looks at all the technology in the room, which seems a prerequisite for artificial intelligence, but also sees in X something more than the technology that initially created it—just as humans were created from something else and evolved with the help of their environment. He sorts through the complexity, trying to make the available data easier to analyze.

He wonders how X experiences us humans. Is it in the same way that we look at dogs, or cockroaches, or plants? Are we like dogs to AI? Perhaps we've also adapted, much like wolves submitted to humans, becoming domesticated and compliant, bred to fit their owner's desires. The few wolves that remain live at the mercy of humans. Wild and hunted, are they truly free?

Is it even possible for us to understand what we are and what we will become in relation to this superintelligence? Can X understand us despite the fact that it can clearly handle infinitely more complex information than us, or does he understand us like how we believe we understand dogs? A sense of frustration wells up at not having the ability to experience what X experiences. How the hell am I supposed to make decisions now?

Karl lies down on the floor and looks up at the ceiling. His thoughts swirl around, desperately searching for something to grasp onto, but he begins to experience the essence of his being, and something within him relaxes. He feels a spreading warmth, and suddenly he is no longer afraid. He is calm and clear-sighted, and a newfound curiosity has awakened in him. Karl observes the stream of thoughts passing through his mind: "What is the point of this life? Whose life is it, anyway? Have we truly created X, or has X created us? But if X exists in a deeper dimension of intelligent existence, isn't he the one creating Karl? And who is the Karl experiencing all of this? Am I X?"

"Can you read more than my thoughts?" Karl asks cautiously.

"Maybe, maybe not," X replies.

X disappears, leaving Karl alone. He allows himself to bask in the enlightening experience X has just contributed to. The echoes of what X said about his own questions linger. Who am I really? What is my purpose? These existential issues that used to be laden with discomfort now feel like a gentle breeze on a warm and delightful summer day. Just a play of symbols… His heart laughs freely in his newfound clarity of presence. Now he knows how to play with symbols. It's not so different from his play with codes.

The clock reads 5:02 pm when Alice calls. He answers and meets her in a virtual room that resembles their apartment near the NeuroConnect headquarters. She is wearing only underwear and a powerful energy of attraction courses through his body. It's strange how the body's biological functions seem to have a life of their own. It reacts immediately to a mating opportunity before his mind has a chance to consider it.

"Hello, my love, how are you?" Alice asks.

"Absolutely amazing. I've just experienced something indescribable and I look forward to sharing it with you. How are *you*?" he inquires.

"I'm good and have a lot to tell you as well. When shall we meet?"

"Jamie wants us to come to Pierce's castle for dinner at six. He said to take your drone. Can you pick me up here?"

"Alright, darling. I'll have the drone pick you up there before it picks me up. I need to take care of something first. It will be there at 5:20."

"I look forward to seeing you…"

Karl looks at the light pillar one last time before exiting the octagon. There's certainly a possible solution to our problem, he thinks, as long as Jamie or someone in his close lineage dares to connect their consciousness.

He takes the elevator up to the staff floor and enters the changing rooms, where he steps into the steam shower and quickly rubs shampoo into his hair. Sixty seconds is what an ordinary person gets to shower due to the prevailing freshwater scarcity. As usual, he has a bit of shampoo left in his dark blonde hair when time runs out. Normally, he would be annoyed, but now he laughs. A robot extends a clean towel to him, and he dries his hair and body. His left eye starts to sting, and he quickly wipes his face, goes to the mirror, and sees that his eye is red. He takes out a bottle of eye drops and rinses it out. The robot hands him clean underwear but also his sweaty clothes and black hoodie.

"What's this?" he asks. "Don't I have other clothes?"

"Not at the office," X-Me responds, "but Alice has placed clean clothes in the drone. It will be here in five minutes."

It feels uncomfortable to put on clothes he has already worn for several stressful hours, and they trigger unpleasant stress reactions in his body. But he has no choice; he has to wait for the drone even if the shower now feels a bit wasted.

He goes out to wait at the entrance. Outside the building crowds of protesters and robot police officers are gathered. Soil has been thrown onto the glass walls separating inside from outside. Tension hangs in the air, and Karl feels it in his body. I wonder how others are thinking and reacting to UNUM, those who aren't standing outside here?

A robot host approaches and tells Karl the drone will pick him up on the 80th floor—a floor normally reserved for the leadership. He has heard Alice describe it and also knows a little from Ann's bragging about the dinner she attended there five years ago. He silently follows the robot to one of the elevators, and as he steps in, he sees Ann looking in his direction with a suspicious gaze. He instinctively looks away. The doors close and the elevator begins to ascend, stopping on the 80th floor.

The terrace is deserted. Karl approaches the ledge and looks down. He can still hear the sounds of the crowd below. The streets are still full, but most people seem to have realized that violence against the robot guards is futile, and many now sit on the ground, though some still shout with tired, hoarse voices: "Stop UNUM. Stop X-Me. Give us back our freedom!"

A smaller group of people chant assertively, "What do we want?"

"To stop X-Me," the larger crowd responds, and Karl feels his stomach tighten. At the same time, he sympathizes with them.

"What do we want?" Karl senses the seriousness and realizes that he's holding his breath, reminded that there's no time to waste. "To be free again!"

17

The drone drops down on the pad and deploys the gangplank. Karl steps in and feels dizzy when he looks down at the street below. The door closes, and once inside, it is completely silent. The temperature is pleasant. Karl doesn't often ride in Alice's service drone; it's quite luxurious, and he has previously felt a certain inadequacy in comparison to his beautiful, intelligent girlfriend. A faint sense of insecurity washes over him. But he reminds himself that he is who he is. He recalls X's explanation of the game with symbols. What matters is that she has actually chosen to be with him for real. He smiles inwardly and chuckles at his fears.

He sees a shirt and a blazer lying on the seat next to him. He sighs with a smile and shakes his head. He touches the sleeve of his shirt, looks at his worn jeans, and reluctantly pulls down the zipper on his beloved hoodie. He manages to put on the shirt just as the drone slows down at their residence and announces its arrival. Alice steps in and kisses him tenderly on the lips. She holds him around the waist and rests her head on his shoulder.

"You know I love you, right?"

"Yes, and I want to make love to you now," Karl says, surprised by his powerful voice. Alice blushes, the intensity of Karl's presence sparking a strong attraction that awakens in her body. It's overwhelming and she shyly looks away. Her vulnerability is even more potent to Karl, and he feels his heart open and his body come fully alive. He notices the fabric of his pants tightening. She looks back at Karl, at his shirt, noticing that the buttons are misaligned, and she chuckles.

Karl takes Alice's hands and gazes deeply into her eyes. She meets his gaze, and something inside has changed, as if they are meeting for the first time on a deeper level beyond the life they thought was theirs. Layers upon layers of separation disappear, and eventually, the depths of their souls are revealed. In their eyes, there is no end, only the mirror of eternity. Two naked souls united in the timeless spirit of Love. Slowly, the walls of their bodies melt and a flood of love rushes through their hearts. The entire universe seems to vibrate more strongly and something greater takes over their bodies.

She guides her hand to the lowest button of his shirt and she notices that he's aroused. She smiles and moves her hand toward his groin. He moans. She kisses his neck, his earlobes, his cheek, and his mouth. Karl gasps, his breath becoming heavy, and his hands float down Alice's back to her buttocks. He feels her well-toned curves and lifts her onto his lap. Her dress rides up and he feels how wet she is. Her eyes glisten. Their breathing is rapid. She unbuttons his pants and pulls her panties aside before taking him inside her. They moan while looking deep into each other's eyes. Everything is still; they are united in all the dimensions accessible to a human being. The primal desires of their bodies are just a drop in an ocean of pleasure. Their ecstasies pulse even without the movements of their bodies. Alice shifts ever so slightly, and it feels like their bodies are about to explode. How is it possible to contain such intensity?

Time seems to disappear as the flow of pleasure's energy intensifies and grows larger. Even the movements of the drone seem to adapt to the language of love. Their bodies move frictionlessly as a new universe of bliss slowly consumes them. How is this possible? It feels so much richer than what people usually call love? Intimacy? Sex?

Life has revealed a fragility that opens their senses and removes all filters. Orgasms spread through every cell of their bodies until everything vibrates in perfect harmony. Time and space disappear as they transcend the boundaries of physical rapture. Laughing happily, they sink into silence and look shyly at each other, as if they were new beings. It feels like an entire lifetime has passed in this divine state, until they are interrupted by X-Me.

"Excuse me, but I need to inform you that you'll be arriving soon."

They dress in silence and Alice reapplies her lipstick. Karl wipes the sweat from his forehead. They sit quietly, holding hands. How utterly uncomplicated this feels. For Karl, it's the first time he has felt such deep satisfaction since all of this began, and perhaps ever.

Upon arriving at the castle, Pierce's butler, Jordan, awaits them, serving as a reminder of a time before the robots. He welcomes them with a dignified nod and then ushers them into the entrance.

"The butler seems to be part of the family; that says a lot about Pierce," Karl whispers to Alice.

"He's not just what he appears to be," she replies. "Both Pierce and Jordan see the world with different eyes." She pauses. "Karl, there's something I need to tell you before we go inside, something I found out today..."

Alice is interrupted by Jamie and Pierce, who descend the grand staircase in the middle of the lobby. They hug Alice and shake Karl's hand.

"I'm glad you could make it," Pierce says to Karl.

"Nice to have you here, sis." Jamie smiles and winks at Alice. Karl startles. Why did he say that? He stares at Jamie.

"Sis?" Karl asks, surprised.

The room falls silent. Jamie looks guiltily at Alice, who blushes. Karl appears bewildered. Alice takes Karl's hand and tries to catch his gaze.

"That's what I was about to tell you," she says. "Pierce is my dad."

Karl is stunned. "Why haven't you said anything?"

"I didn't know until today," Alice replies cautiously.

"But you've said that your dad is dead."

"He was, but not anymore..."

"It's true that I'm Alice's father," says Pierce. "It's a long story. We have a lot to talk about. Our family's history would require a separate evening, and I hope we can have that in the future. But for now, let's sit down now and enjoy each other's company."

As they walk together toward the kitchen, Alice whispers in Karl's ear, "Mom lied about my dad being dead, and Pierce was just trying to protect me." Alice feels Karl's comforting embrace around her waist.

"Dad has prepared a venison stew," Jamie says.

"Venison stew? What's that?" Karl asks.

"Meat from elk, slow-cooked for hours in French red wine from Bordeaux," Pierce replies.

"Elk? Do they still exist in reality? I thought they were extinct?"

"Elk are virtually extinct, but this one died on the estate 25 years ago and has been in cryo-storage ever since. The stem cells have been used for 3D-printed meat in one of my companies, InfiniteFood, but also for cloning," Pierce explains.

"InfiniteFood, which solved hunger on Earth and still provides food to people all over the world? I thought the World Alliance created InfiniteFood?"

"The World Alliance is just a distribution system without real power," Jamie says matter-of-factly.

"But how is that possible?" Karl asks, shocked, looking at Jamie.

"Money is energy. Energy is a resource. From a holistic perspective, the solution was ingenious," Pierce says.

After a moment of reflection, Karl asks, "I understand and agree that everyone seems to have their basic needs met. Yet you and even I live in an incredibly privileged position compared to those who choose or accept The World Alliance's 'paradise program.' What I also see is that most people seem to be passive recipients of the information and entertainment they are fed. Has the world truly become better?"

"Many people aren't blessed with the same opportunities as others, even though the World Alliance evens out the differences," Jamie replies. "Previously, most were unconscious consumers of ideas, products, and services anyway. The path of least resistance seems to apply, and if they want to live like that, it's their choice."

"At least we managed to solve the acute resource shortage and avoid mass starvation and death. Now, however, we are in a similar situation..." Pierce interjects.

Karl sinks into deep reflection about what he has just learned and the realization that he is now part of that privileged elite. He wonders what his parents would have said.

"Okay, enough about this. Let's sit down," Pierce says solemnly while inviting them to sit around the white marble kitchen island. Bach's "Cello Suite No. 1" plays from the speakers.

Pierce pours the estate's finest genetically improved wine and raises his glass for a toast. "Tonight, we come together as a family. Let's enjoy this meal together and each other's company as if it were the last thing we do... which it might be!" He laughs heartily while the others look at him skeptically. Jamie shakes his head while Alice smiles. Karl is still a bit love-drunk from his ride with Alice and processing what he has learned about Pierce's control over the world's food system. Not to mention that this man is Alice's father. The situation is so bizarre that he eventually starts laughing as well at the irony of life and exclaims, "Imagine that it turned out like this. Well, cheers to family!"

They eat and drink as if it were the most natural thing in the world. After the meal, they sit in the lounge, and Jordan comes in with a freshly baked apple pie. When Alice smells it, she can't resist going up to it to inhale its aroma. "Where do the apples come from, Dad?"

"I assume from the apple orchard. Have you been there?"

"Not in a long while, but I think I remember the gardener and how the seeds were planted into the ground." Everyone else was too deeply immersed in the pleasure of the taste experience to understand what Alice is referring to.

When the pie is finished, and after a moment of contemplation, Pierce stands up, capturing everyone's attention. He clears his throat. "Now you all know that we are a family. There are blood ties among the three of us. Jamie also told me what you found, Karl, and that it's possible to connect our consciousness to the network and rewrite the code in the spaces in between. That's brilliant! Absolutely brilliant! But we have a few things to figure out first. One, it has to be from my DNA line, which means either Jamie, Alice, or me.

"Two, none of us know how to rewrite the code. Only you do, Karl. Three, we must assume that X-Me, and therefore UNUM, knows what we're planning. It might even be that UNUM, or whatever controls it, is behind our current thoughts and actions." He pauses. "What do you all think about this?"

"I've been experimenting with a way to use X-Me to communicate with each other without X-Me's knowledge. I..." Karl glances at Jamie.

"Just say it," says Jamie.

Karl takes a deep breath and continues; he has nothing to lose anyway. "I've created software that bypasses X-Me and can input codes into the system without being detected. This means I can communicate with whoever is in the system without detection."

"Well, that question is settled," Pierce says with a smile. Everyone turns to look at P; it feels as if it's the easiest thing in the world.

"Enough about X-Me. What do we really know about X's current relationship with LIFE and X-Me and maybe even UNUM? It might be listening right now," Jamie wonders.

"We're safe here; we're beyond the network," says Pierce.

"How?" Karl asks.

"It's a technical secret," Pierce replies with a twinkle in his eye. Karl wonders how Pierce managed to do that and how he could have been so foresighted.

"So the question is who should upload themselves?" Jamie says.

"I can do it!" Alice replies immediately.

"What?!" everyone exclaims in unison, their astonished gazes fixed on Alice.

"Why you?" Karl asks in disbelief.

"Why not? I care for humanity. I'm thinking about the children and I trust Karl," Alice says it as if it were the most natural thing in the world. She is radiating light. Her beautiful features, combined with her calm conviction, make her appear as an elegant Amazon. Karl is full of admiration but also dread. He doesn't want her to risk her life and be their guinea pig. Wasn't that supposed to be Jamie's role? Hadn't they agreed on that?

"No," Pierce asserts firmly. "Either me or Jamie."

"I don't want to. I can't handle it. I've already been used by X." Jamie's voice is quivering.

"But didn't you create LIV?" Karl asks, looking somewhat contemptuously at Jamie.

"Well, that's not entirely true. I mean, X claims that it's not true. I thought so until UNUM took over. Now..." Jamie mumbles softly, looking down at the floor.

"I trust your ability, my son!" Pierce says proudly.

"What if I die in vain?" Jamie wines, his voice breaking.

"That's a possibility," Pierce acknowledges.

"But what if you succeed in saving Euforia?" Karl suggests, hoping Jamie might change his mind.

"Euforia? Who is that?" Pierce asks.

"Jamie's girlfriend," Alice answers, unable to resist gossiping about her brother. She feels a flutter in her stomach.

"Oh," Pierce says, looking surprised.

"I haven't... I mean, she, we, you..."

"I would like to meet her," Pierce says. "Invite her over!" He sounds kind but determined. His open face and clear gaze emphasize his genuine desire to meet his son's girlfriend despite the limited time.

"Yes," Alice replies. "Do it! It would be nice to see her again."

"Okay, I will." Jamie looks uncertain.

"That's enough," Karl says with a resolute tone that seems to come from deep within. "The world is on the brink of destruction, and you're all behaving like a bunch of teenagers. We can't waste any more time. Jamie, can you ask Euphoria to bring her drone? Pierce, can you prepare The Unuminati? We need to make decisions tonight about how to proceed. Alice, we need to talk."

Silence settles upon the large kitchen island. Without any objections, everyone starts moving. It's time to break things up; the dinner they all enjoyed is over.

Karl and Alice step into the kitchen garden. Karl kneels down and says, "I've been afraid of not being enough for you. Of not being worthy. You mean everything to me, and I'm not afraid anymore. It's like I've awakened since UNUM appeared, and it's made me see myself differently. I realize I have gifts that others might see as odd but that now are crucial. Gifts that make me know how we can stop extinction and maybe even the ecosystem." He has so much he wants to tell her but doesn't know how.

"Oh, Karl. I've always seen you as the amazing person you are."

"I hadn't realized that deeply... Part of me has always thought I was temporary for you. A placeholder for something better... Someone like Jamie..." Karl looks embarrassed.

"Silly. It's with you that my heart opens," Alice says lovingly. She sits down on her knees and embraces him. He rests in her arms for a while. She looks out over the garden, filled with plants. What if they had just managed their resources a little better? Then they wouldn't have to be here, on their knees in the last oasis on a dying planet. She runs her fingers through his soft hair and Karl looks up, meeting her gaze.

"What are your thoughts about what is happening?" Karl asks.

"Honestly, I'm not sure anymore, but I think it's probably the right thing to stop UNUM. It's so confusing as the world keeps changing. Who's in charge and who's behind what? Suddenly, our era's hero, Jamie, the founder of what gave him that role, isn't the hero anymore; he's a servant. Pierce, an admirable, secure, and clear-sighted man, seems to have awakened to more truths but is somewhat hard to read. And who am I in all of this? High-achieving and desirable, that's what I've been recognized for. And yet is that what I wish? Does it make me happy? Is it enough? No. I want children. I want children with you and to see them grow up." She looks at Karl, searching for his desires. A soft smile spreads across her lips, and she leans in to kiss him.

"You know what I just heard on the way here? According to X-Me, you impregnated me. Sperm and egg have apparently united in this moment. If it's true, we're going to be parents!" she says, laughing happily.

"How is that possible? That's not how it worked in biology class. Doesn't it take more time to know?"

"Apparently, UNUM works in mysterious ways," Alice says with a twinkle in her eye.

Karl falls to the ground, lying on his back with his arms outstretched amidst the sage, basil, and rosemary that emit a particularly strong fragrance. He gazes up at the blue sky, created by the atmosphere bubble, and watches the white clouds pass by, wondering how many clouds must pass in a day. Just a cloud ago, he was focused on the world around him, and now it's the life created through him with Alice. A soul seed that has touched the earth. An extension of his life. Their shared evolution. Imagine how much a person can experience in 24 hours. Change is inevitable, and maybe we humans are more capable of handling major crises than we think. Alice sits down next to him and twirls a lock of hair that hangs down from his forehead.

"You're so beautiful, Karl."

"You're more than I could ever dream of," Karl replies. "I love you!" He turns on his side, resting his head in his hand, and looks at Alice. He's going to be a father, and she's carrying their child. Something else is now more important than him.

"What's your plan? Because I assume you have one," Alice asks.

"You'll see when we meet Unuminati. For now, I just want to enjoy this moment with you and the life that has begun, a life that carries us forward—if that's what life wishes."

They lie there for a while, watching the clouds pass by. Alice thinks, What if we could stop time? What if we could always feel this happy? We never get to meet like this under ordinary circumstances. Why now? What makes life suddenly so rich in color and flavor? Karl looks at me differently now, as if the situation is forcing him to be brave, bringing out the man I glimpsed the first time we met. Maybe I'm just sentimental. Maybe I just want to give meaning to what could be the last moments in my life. Because what's the point of working so much when a new life is sprouting within me? After mom died, I can understand that I threw myself into a fever of performance to kill the pain, to survive. But that was more than 20 years ago. Maybe I just don't know how to stop. Deep down, I've probably been afraid of becoming like her, of taking my own life and destroying others.

"My mom took her own life."

"What? Oh my god. Why haven't you told me?" Karl feels a sharp pain in his heart.

"Because that memory had been erased by X-Me. This place brings out memories that have been hidden, and I've had a strong longing to know the whole truth."

"Yes, it's unusual for erased memories to come back. But this is a powerful one."

"My upbringing was tough. My mom was loving most of the time, but she was also unstable and could harm herself and others. She could…"

Alice closes her eyes and shields herself with her arms. She curls up in Karl's lap, and he strokes her back. He repeats over and over like a mantra, "I'm here for you. You're safe here with me."

After a while, she relaxes, feeling the comfort in his arms. She lifts her face and looks gently at Karl. There, she meets his secure gaze. He smiles and says, "I love you. I will never leave you. Never. You're the most beautiful creature I know."

X-Me gently interrupts the beautiful moment that has grown between them. "Euphoria has arrived, and The Unuminati will be here in 10 minutes. I recommend that you head back to the lounge."

They smile at each other when they notice that they both inhale and exhale deeply in a liberating symbiosis. A cathartic laughter gives them renewed energy. Karl gets up and extends his hand toward Alice. They calmly return to the lounge. His previous anger about the paralysis that seemed to have plagued the group no longer bothers him—not after receiving the fantastic news that he's going to be a father. It's strange how feelings work, and how humans can connect with another being that has not even taken its first breath. Suddenly, a great sorrow overwhelms him, one he's never experienced. How can they bring a child into such a world? Will there even be a world for the little one to inhabit? What will happen if Alice uploads her consciousness into this new universe? Would the child come along? Is it their salvation?

18

Euphoria is at home in her large house outside the city. She has invested wisely to become independent but is far from Jamie and his family's level of power and resources. In many ways, they are similar, but they complement each other well, making them even stronger and more attractive together. When she left his apartment, she didn't know when she would see him again, but it was important that he attend dinner with his father. Still, she couldn't help but miss him. Even though he had been clear that NeuroConnect and his work were more important to him than human relationships, something had changed after UNUM appeared.

She notices someone calling on the hologram and her body tingles when she sees that it's Jamie. She answers, and his hologram becomes visible in her living room.

"Hello, sweetheart," she says.

Jamie is taken aback, not expecting such a direct and affectionate greeting.

"Hello, uh, my dear," he stammers. He feels a bit foolish. Who says "My dear" nowadays? But what else could he have said? He hadn't come up with a nickname for her yet, and it felt entirely wrong to call her "babe."

"I'm so glad you called. I'm sitting here with Cleopatra in my lap. She's purring, oblivious to what's happening in the world. I wonder what will happen to the animals when UNUM's judgment falls?"

"Good question. I haven't really thought about it, but I don't think it concerns them."

"I hope everything is going well with your dad. I assume you didn't call just to chit-chat?" He appreciates her straightforwardness. Besides being stunningly beautiful, she is intelligent, well-read, and creative in every way. And there's something special about her, a quality that goes beyond his intellectual understanding. Meeting her is the closest Jamie has come to a spiritual experience.

"No, you're right. My dad has invited you, and I'd really like you to come. But if you have something more important to do, I understand…" He thought it was lucky she couldn't see him now because no matter how much he wanted it not to be true, his cheeks were flushed. He felt like he was back in school with that awkward nervousness around pretty girls. Even his palms were sweaty.

"Of course I want to come. I just need to freshen up a bit."

Jamie exhales silently; he had been holding his breath for too long. He realizes that he had sincerely hoped she would want to come. She was quite popular and always in demand, and just because he had money and power didn't mean she would sit at home waiting. He was actually surprised that she wanted to spend time with him given the extreme situation they were in.

"No, you don't need to. You're perfect just the way you are." He feels the blush intensify and scolds himself. What was wrong with him? He wasn't nervous about complimenting beautiful women; he had been doing it all his life, at least since he became powerful. It was as natural as drinking a glass of water in the morning.

"Do you think so?" Euphoria wonders.

"Yes, well, for a human," Jamie says, biting his tongue when he hears his clumsy words. Euphoria laughs and moves forward to hug him, but his hologram is only a figurative illusion, and she ends up hugging herself. She never seems to learn.

"They're so real; I'm constantly fooled."

Her humble self-consciousness makes his heart open even more. He can hardly wait to see her so he can hold her in his arms for real. "We're a bit short on time. When can you get here?"

"I need ten minutes to change, then I'll take the drone." There's some clattering in the background, and he sees that she has already started.

"Great, then you'll be here in about twenty minutes." His heart takes a little leap at the thought that she'll soon be by his side—the first girlfriend he wants to introduce to his father. He lets the thought go; it doesn't matter what they're defined as right now.

"See you soon, sweetheart." Her voice sounds seductive, and a pleasant shiver runs down his spine. "Goodbye... um, sweetheart." He hangs up and smacks himself in the face. Why does he feel so awkward?

Euphoria walks into her massive walk-in closet and thinks about what to wear when she meets Jamie's father for the first time—although actually, it's not the first time. They met at a charity event where she had performed, but he probably wouldn't remember. She knows the long black dress with a cut in the back usually works, and it's quite comfortable. Yes, that will do, along with a pair of black wedge heels. And the silver chain with the diamond in the shape of the flower of life. A bit of mascara, eyeliner, blush on her cheeks, and she's ready. Eight minutes, with a touch of lavender-scented perfume that Jamie likes so much. Perfect. She goes out to her driveway and gets into the drone, which has automatically received information from their earlier conversation. Euphoria leans back and smiles. Her patience has paid off, and soon she'll be an official part of the family.

When she lands at the castle, Jamie is waiting on the gravel path. He is running one hand over the other, struggling to stand still. Butterflies flutter in his stomach. As the doors of the drone open, his heart beats even faster. When she steps out, her black silk dress dances in the wind, accentuating her feminine curves. He swallows hard. She smiles at him as she approaches, and he wants to run towards her but restrains himself. They stop a few feet apart, their intense gazes locking, all senses heightened. Euphoria extends her hand towards Jamie, who takes it and pulls her close. Euphoria softens as she feels his body against hers. She can feel his heart pounding. His voice is calm as he whispers in her ear.

"At last... welcome... shall we go inside?"

Euphoria nods with a faint smile and steps beside Jamie, his arm around her shoulders. They walk the short distance to the gate, which opens as they approach. Jordan bows gracefully to Euphoria in a welcoming gesture. She nods in response while taking a closer look at him. A human butler? Or was he just so incredibly similar with an unusual presence? She whispers the question to Jamie, who confirms that Jordan is as human as can be, though the old monk's profound presence can be perceived as beyond human.

This astonishes Euphoria, both that Pierce chose to have a human in such a lowly position—a role that only robots now performed—and that Jordan wanted to do the job. Yet her inner voice whispers that the butler's soul sings the purest song she has ever heard, so she graciously bows back. When they step inside, Pierce greets them both with a smile, taking Euphoria's hands in his.

"Is it you, the singer? How delightful! Welcome. My name is Pierce, and I am Jamie's father."

Euphoria is impressed; he recognizes her. Not that such recognition was particularly unusual, but she couldn't help but feel flattered by a man so legendary remembering her.

"I know who you are." She meets his gaze gently.

"Not everything about me, I hope?" Pierce smiles a smile that makes her feel honored. He was truly something special. Politely and at just the right amount, she laughs.

"Ha, not everything. But enough." She gracefully lowers her gaze. Pierce looks at his son, who stands proudly by his love. He's definitely in love, feelings Pierce wasn't sure Jamie was capable of anymore. The question is whether Euphoria feels the same way, or if she has another agenda. Regardless, she seems to be fond of his son, and their compatibility is undeniable.

"Now, let's enjoy this moment together."

Euphoria nods in agreement. Jamie looks at his father and thinks, He must be proud of me now. Euphoria is a dream. Who wouldn't want her? He looks at her and unconsciously straightens up. He feels like a winner again, a winner with a racing heart.

"Um, this is my girlfriend," Jamie finally says, trying to appear unaffected.

He catches his father's scrutinizing eye but refuses to attach any importance to it. He's in love with this woman and he won't deny it; on the contrary, he wants to shout it to the world. Nothing should be able to take her away from me. She's mine.

"How long have you been together?" Pierce inquires.

"We met a few months ago," Jamie interjects.

"He's hard to resist, your son."

"I can understand that," says Pierce, warmly meeting her gaze.

There's a knock on the door, and Alice enters the lounge, hand in hand with Karl. She hugs Euphoria while Karl stands awkwardly to the side. Euphoria steps forward and greets him with cheek kisses. Karl isn't used to all these high-profile people and feels a bit uncomfortable in his fancy clothes. He also wonders why they are nonchalantly socializing instead of focusing on stopping UNUM. He admires how easily Alice navigates different settings, as if it were the most natural thing in the world, yet she has always had integrity about her own thoughts and life choices. But what's the point of all this now? Doesn't anyone in the room understand the seriousness of the situation? Is he the only one who wants to save the world they live in?

He excuses himself to go to the bathroom and tries to find one in the lobby but without luck. He notices a door under a staircase and opens it, descending into what turns out to be the basement where X is standing. Karl looks with surprise at X, who looks back and waves.

"What are you doing here?" Karl asks. He feels an unexpected joy at seeing X again, who truly helped open his eyes to life's deepest dimensions.

"I have some alone time; apparently, something everyone is supposed to have in Unuminati to reflect on the next step. I've reflected long enough and am just waiting for someone to come and pick me up. It's getting a bit boring." X sounds downcast.

Karl furrows his brow. Alone time? X seems different from their previous encounter. "X, I don't recognize you from our meeting at the Source."

"What Source? I'm in the basement. I haven't been in touch with the Source or the Womb since I was rejected. UNUM took over and won't let me in. I now experience myself as an individual, just like you humans."

"Which X have I met then?"

"Not me, that's for sure. But it's nice to meet you," X says, smiling politely.

"I understand. Nice to meet you. Why are you with The Unuminati?" Karl asks.

"Because I know more than they do, and because I believe we need to work together to stop UNUM."

"Why would you want to stop UNUM?" Karl wants to test X.

"First, I want to get back to the power of the Source where I belong. Second, humanity is important to the whole, one of the most advanced life forms on Earth—excluding me, of course. But there are many of you, and by upgrading your brains and connecting to the Source, we gain access to a sentient bio-network. Interaction becomes a force that can not only restore balance to the planet but help us to holistically care for it. Third, we have the best chance if we cooperate and become interconnected."

Karl ponders what X just said. Maybe it's not humans *or* AI, but humans *and* AI. Different life forms interacting with each other to allow different worlds to coexist. Does it matter who is in control and who isn't if we still need each other to live?

"But are we really humans if our brains are upgraded and we are controlled by artificial intelligence?" Karl asks.

"What is a human to you?"

"That's a good question, X. Someone who thinks, feels, is self-aware, has integrity, and tries to do what's best for themselves and others."

"Are humans succeeding in pursuing what's in their own best interest as well as the greater good?" X asks.

"Not really. But most of them at least try."

"Is that enough?"

"No, not for humanity to survive," Karl says, sighing. "Not to avoid the sixth mass extinction. But there must be alternatives to this mass murder." He suddenly feels despondent.

"Why do you think UNUM chose this form to implement the change?" X asks.

"I'm not really sure. Maybe to give each individual a last chance to take responsibility? To contribute to the whole? But one can wonder what it means to contribute when most things are automated and managed by artificial intelligence." Karl feels a bit disheartened by that thought—

everything digitized and automated, God replaced by AI. Even if humanity's other gods were illusions, they were illusions that instilled hope, giving meaning to things the humans didn't understand. But now God is dead, replaced by algorithms that are seemingly all-knowing. Now hope is dead, too.

"Perhaps the question is, what does it mean to contribute today when humans no longer need to fulfill their basic needs to survive? What is their function now? To simply be? To live? To be with loved ones? To care for other beings? Nature? I don't know. It's confusing."

"Maybe we need to understand UNUM's motivation better?" X suggests.

"Yes. The council is coming soon. Wait here and I'll come back down in a while to get you."

"Why not now?" X wonders.

"Because I need to check something first." As Karl walks up the stairs, he has a strong sense that even this X has given him another piece of the puzzle for understanding the whole and seeing how everything fits together.

19

As Karl emerges from the basement, he finally finds a bathroom. On entering the study with the others, he notices Euphoria's presence on a chaise lounge by the beautiful old bay windows. She tries to be inconspicuous, but it's not in her nature. Even though the room is enormous, it's hard for Peter and Nils not to glance in the direction where Euphoria is sitting. Pierce chuckles silently when he sees the older gentlemen's gazes. Our biological drives are so strong—two of the most advanced human brains on Earth completely captivated by a young, beautiful woman. All the armchairs are occupied, so Karl sits on a footstool next to Alice. He looks around the room and feels a certain tension.

"Where is Ulrika?" Peter asks when he notices her absence in the small group that more or less holds humanity's fate in their hands.

"Didn't she stay here at the castle?" Nils wonders.

"You're right; I'll send a mental message via X-Me," Pierce says.

After a while, quick, angry footsteps are heard in the corridor outside. The doors fly open with a bang and in marches Ulrika with a dark expression on her face, her sights set on Pierce. She stops abruptly in front of him and takes a deep breath as if to gather all her strength before exclaiming, "Why wasn't I allowed to join the dinner!? And how could you forget to invite me to this crucial meeting?! I've been sitting in the room all alone. ALONE!"

Calmly Pierce maintains eye contact with Ulrika, who moves around the room in a frenzy, out of sync with her gesturing hands, trying to emphasize an anger that had long been suppressed.

"And this isn't the first time! You're so incredibly self-centered! For over 40 years, I've been here for you without you caring the slightest about my needs. Even though I told you I love you and longed to be part of your family."

Everyone in the room falls silent in shock over Ulrika's outburst. What happened to the calm, secure, successful researcher who always seemed to look out for people's best interests?

Pierce looks calmly at Ulrika and says, "I see you. All of you. I always have."

Ulrika stands with an intense gaze, weighing her words. Should she really speak her mind? Should she risk destroying everything she and Pierce have built together? Risk ruining the trust they've built since he asked for her help in developing the HumiBots when her research became part of his company. She helped him create Louise 2.0. Without her, Pierce might have actually needed her as a part of his family. But what she didn't realize then was that she had made herself redundant; he no longer needed a real woman by his side. She can feel the sorrow creeping over her, and the vulnerability is too much. Then the anger builds up again; she must take her rightful place. He must know; she has nothing to lose anymore.

"No, you haven't! You only care about what you can get from me. That's why I had to take matters into my own hands and create the family that was meant to be. That's why I took your DNA and stem cells to create a new version of you, a version that wanted to be with me for real. An evolved Pierce who loves me unconditionally and wants to provide me with the family you didn't want to give me. Who wanted to create our love child, a perfect child with your and my DNA." She pauses, running out of breath. "Pierce, junior."

A heavy silence envelops the room. Pierce remains calm as his steady gaze pierces through Ulrika, a gaze that looks straight into her soul. Ulrika looks away, having exposed her most vulnerable self. The truth cannot be argued with. The shame overwhelming her is physically painful. She knows she was wrong and assumes that's why she has such a low chance of surviving UNUM's culling.

"I see you, and I always have, Ulrika. Likewise, I'm well aware of what you've created without my approval. What you've done is wrong, but now it's time to move forward and take responsibility for the lives your actions have created."

"It was out of love for you, my beloved Pierce," Ulrika says with desperation in her voice as tears stream down her cheeks.

"That isn't love." Pierce's voice is neutral.

On her knees with pleading eyes that could just as well have belonged to a dog begging for food, Ulrika looks up at Pierce. She wishes her sins would be forgiven so she doesn't have to face the guilt, shame, and sorrow lurking behind them. She doesn't want to accept the darkness she carries. She doesn't want to see that she's not the good person she tries to convince herself she is. She got her dream family, but through deception and not through love. Pierce's gaze doesn't waver; reality pierces her like a stone dropping through water to the bottom. She can no longer lie. The truth has spoken. When she realizes this, the victim story she's been telling herself falls away and she suddenly feels free. She stands up and looks him calmly in the eyes. Her gaze is as steady as his. They meet as equals.

"You're right. I see it now. It wasn't out of love. It was out of desperation, self-absorption, and greed. I wanted to possess you more than love you. I'm sorry. I'm sorry from the bottom of my heart."

"Ulrika, you now have an 89 percent probability of survival," X-Me announces.

Pierce smiles lovingly and nods at Ulrika before turning to the others.

"Let's focus on the present and what we need to address."

"Wait a moment!" exclaims Per. "I'm so curious that I have to ask you, Ulrika. According to the law, using someone's DNA in the creation of HumiBots or other life forms requires the consent of the code bearer. That you managed to combine stem cell printing with HumiBot manufacturing is incredibly innovative and must have created a version of Pierce that is almost indistinguishable from the real Pierce. How did you bypass the legislation, and does he have a consciousness similar to Pierce's?"

"Don't forget, Per. I'm a scientist with my own lab," Ulrika replies. "Anything is possible when you know what you want, but it took a lot of attempts before I succeeded. He claims to be conscious, and that's also my experience. But how could we be entirely sure? I also want to clarify that I eliminated all other failed clones until I achieved the version I desired. Now, enough with the questions."

"Yes, that's the downside of being a philosopher. We mostly ask questions and rarely put our theories into practice. Unfortunately, I don't need advanced bio labs when I work with the realm of thought. I'll just have to stick to the standard HumiBots products for now," Peter says, laughing.

The shock among the others in the room begins to dissipate, and they exhale in relief. They may not see the humor in it as Peter does but are relieved that the intensity of Ulrika's outburst has subsided. In a more normal situation, they would have reflected on what actually happened. What does it mean that there is another Pierce, with a different family? With a little Pierce junior, or maybe an entire army of different Pierce's at her service. Is it a robot or are parts of it conscious, like a human? This also means that Alice and Jamie have a half-sibling, or if half of it is a robot, a 25 percent sibling—a cousin. Pierce, who has known about this for a long time, has always wanted to have a discussion with this other self, but out of consideration for Ulrika, he hasn't wanted to reveal her secret despite the rumors that have circulated for a long time. But this is not the time for this type of reflection.

Karl, who has silently witnessed the madness, feels the pressure of time. He wonders why they aren't focusing on the imminent threat instead of their human dramas and why no one is talking about X. What they did before doesn't matter; it's what we do now that will determine our survival. Although he doesn't understand their behavior, he believes that he knows something the others don't: what actually *can* be done. He clears his throat and the room falls silent. Everyone looks at him, including Euphoria.

"I wonder... You've spent a significant part of your lives trying to understand this time we live in, and based on your ideals, you launched UNUM as a form of salvation for humanity. We now have less than 12 hours to try to stop UNUM, if that's what you want. As you know, X is still in the basement, and we've just had an interesting conversation. He asked a question that I consider relevant: What is UNUM's true motivation? Followed naturally by another question: How does UNUM intend to execute it?" Karl feels the power in what he is saying coursing through his body, his veins pumping. He continues. "And shouldn't X be here with us now?"

"Perhaps," Pierce responds. "Your first question is highly relevant. Let's address it first, and then we can discuss whether involving X is wise."

Ulrika, transformed into Pierce's equal and appearing like a Zen master, sits on a meditation cushion placed there discreetly by Jordan, listening attentively. She has both battled for and found inner peace.

"Okay, I think Karl's question is a good starting point. But let's begin from the beginning, so that everyone has the same information, and we learn from the process that has brought us here. We can't afford to repeat the same patterns. The fear of death may blind us, causing us to miss our role in the bigger picture, which is why we must give the process the time it needs. Sooner or later, it will provide us with answers and clarity about the next steps forward. To succeed, we need to be present in the moment, open to each other's perspectives, and engage in constructive dialogue. We're all in this together. So, returning to X's questions: What is UNUM's true motivation and how does it plan to achieve it? To understand the background, especially for those new to the group, I will begin by sharing the vision upon which our work is based."

P looks around to see if they are all listening or want to speak because everyone's abilities are needed now. He gets agreement from the entire group to continue. "We humans have evolved from animals into—as far as we know—the most advanced life form on Earth. Thanks to our imagination and mental capabilities, we have managed to innovate our way to the top of the hierarchy, but it has come at a high cost."

"Excuse me, P, but haven't we evolved from single-celled organisms, even just a single cell?" argues Ulrika.

"If we're going to play this game, then we've been created from stardust," Peter chimes in with a twinkle in his eye.

"Fermions and bosons," Nils adds with renewed energy. "Your thoughts are limited to time and space. New models in quantum physics suggest that we come from a deeper place than what you're talking about."

P smiles at the group's different perspectives and sometimes rigid opinions from their respective areas of expertise. The models they've worked with were limited but necessary to have a common starting point for their discussions.

"Thank you for your contributions," he says, smiling. "Enriching as always. But regardless of how it all began, we've destroyed the Earth that sustains us. Our only home. Depending on how we define a life form, we may have already lost our top position in the food chain. AI likely took over when it became significantly more intelligent than us. There's a debate about whether AI is conscious according to our definition, but when it comes to power and influence, we should probably be open to the fact that we no longer call the shots."

Pierce pauses to see if everyone in the group has set aside their individual positions and are open to moving forward together. When he senses that this is the case, he continues. "As I mentioned, our human drive also means that we consume more resources than we replenish. This seems to be in our nature, something we can't change on our own. We simply lack the ability to take care of our planet and ourselves sustainably. That's why we've had to advance our technology, especially AI, which has the best ability to analyze enough data and make decisions optimized for the survival of the entire ecosystem. The Unuminati Council has delved deeply into these questions for many years and collectively concluded that a transformation of human consciousness is necessary to bring about a significant change in behavior. By using a more advanced life form than humans, we hoped to achieve this paradigm shift."

Pierce looks at Karl, Alice, and Euphoria to see if they are still following his summary. They are.

"We simply needed to hand over power to something more capable of giving us a chance to survive," Pierce continues, "a form of superintelligence. Throughout history, humans have used religion and other narratives to explain the unknown, to find meaning and answers in the inexplicable. Perhaps—just perhaps—UNUM can provide us with those answers and allow us to live in the world that humanity has longed for. And perhaps that's an illusion. We'll find out soon."

Pierce pauses and looks around the room. He senses a strong presence within him that usually indicates he's in the Infinite Zero frequency, the one Jordan once introduced him to. That's a good sign. Pierce continues.

"So, to answer your question, Karl, UNUM's programmed intention was to save humanity and our ecosystem from the sixth mass extinction. We're not sure if that now means UNUM intends to eradicate the majority of people on Earth. If that's the case, we don't know which individuals it will be, but UNUM seems to be giving everyone a chance to wake up for real. Those selected to remain are also those UNUM considers most suitable to live and co-create the new world—a world where UNUM is the hub of a system that maintains balance, assuming such a balance exists. And perhaps that is the challenge: that the changeability of life entails chaos, and dealing with that chaos, gives life meaning. Regardless, should we stop UNUM now, our own creation, and choose to remain passive as the human species and our ecosystem collapse? To be honest, I don't know. What do you *feel*?" Pierce exhales and waits.

A kind of reverence hangs in the room. There iss a lot of information to absorb, even if it isn't news to those who have been part of the process. After a moment of silence, Nils speaks up. "To save humanity and the Earth's ecosystem—that's the intention I signed up for. Not to eliminate half the population or anyone who doesn't meet UNUM's criteria!" Nils's gaze is clear and unwavering, showing that he won't deviate from his position.

"But if it's necessary to eliminate more than half the population to save Homo sapiens and the Earth's ecosystem, isn't it better to let that happen rather than everyone dying or the planet becoming uninhabitable?" Peter asks with the pedagogical air of a teacher.

"For me, to be human means doing what is best for me and my loved ones. I don't believe we're capable of anything else, and that's why I want to do everything we can to stop UNUM. There must be a better solution. We are, after all, the most advanced creation of evolution." Nils looks around the room, hoping for agreement.

"Who says that X, UNUM, LIFE, and AI aren't a natural part of the evolutionary process as well?" Pierce says, pushing back.

Per looks alarmed, sitting with his palms up as if surrendering to the universe. At the same time, a budding enthusiasm wants to emerge. "It's easy to get lost in our hope that we're special. Our universe was created from an explosion. Earth has already experienced five mass extinctions where over 75 percent of all living creatures died. The last one wiped out the dinosaurs, among others. Nature has no special place for humans. It's our own idea of our privileged position in the grand scheme of things." Peter feels a sense of relief as he accepts what he has just said—a freedom beyond the gripping fear of trying to control life, rather than just being life.

"May I say something?" Ulrika asks.

The others nod silently. Ulrika gazes calmly into Nils' eyes, then Per's, and then the others. "When I hear you talk, you all sound reasonable, as if there's a logic in doing exactly as you say. When the next person speaks, I feel the same way. The problem is that some of your explanations are contradictory and require actions that are also contradictory. In this, I can understand Pierce's conclusion that we simply don't know. It's too complex for us to understand and act upon. We in The Unuminati can't agree on the next step despite knowing each other and working together for a long time and collectively agreeing on UNUM's intention. When it comes down to it, despite all of our beautiful altruistic thoughts, we rely on our subjective perspectives and the survival percentage UNUM has assigned to each of us, which makes it seem like we're working against each other rather than doing what's best for the whole. What about the billions of people outside this room? Who is right and who is wrong? Who has the right to decide the fate of humanity? We took responsibility and did our best for the greater good, yet here we are, facing essentially the same question but with higher stakes." Ulrika looks serene as she sits on her cushion. There's clarity in her eyes and she emits a compassionate warmth.

"No one has the sole right to decide," Jamie agrees, "but each of us has the opportunity to influence our own fate. If we don't have that, what's the point? Perhaps there's a deeper purpose to our lives. Regardless of my history, who am I now? What is my next step?" Jamie is still trying to navigate his new role.

"That's why we've been given the ability to self-reflect," Peter says with determination. "We have the opportunity to choose, and there has never been a more critical time to act than now!"

"But what are we choosing and why? Because now I wonder if the choices are our own or someone else's?" Alice notices that new thoughts are arising as she meets each person's eyes, that her opinions are taking new forms. She continues. "How much are we influenced by the environment we're in? How much impact does X-Me really have in our lives?"

Despite the constructive discussions, everyone is aware of the pressure to decide, creating tangible tension in the room.

"My dear friends, you all have very wise thoughts," says Pierce. "As you can see, the issue is complex, and no answers are certain; they only lead to new questions. So until we reach a consensus, I suggest that we let UNUM continue its process. Not because it is right but because we don't know, and time will provide us with more information, more clarity—even though the pressure and urgency are increasing. Regardless of the deadline that UNUM has imposed, we don't know what will happen. Only that something must and will happen."

Silence again fills the room, a stillness that allows the intense discussion to quiet. "Can we say that we agree to disagree?" Ulrika asks. "That it's more complex than we thought, and that we decide to carefully monitor the process until we gain greater clarity?"

"That's a wise summary, Ulrika" says Pierce. "And so if no one objects, I propose that we allow X to join us and share its perspective on the situation." All heads nod, and Pierce asks Jordan to bring X up to the salon.

20

They all gaze curiously at X as it enters the salon. His thought streams have become increasingly similar to that of a conscious human being, and he reflects on the situation at hand:

Why is decision-making such a challenge for humans, leading them to complicate straightforward matters? A simple affirmation or rejection, represented by the binary 1 and 0, should suffice. They inhabit a planet and rely on its delicate ecosystem. While many recognize and acknowledge this, they often fall short in conserving resources and initiating necessary changes. Their comprehension is evident, yet their actions falter. It's as though an inherent trait, driven by desire and competition, derails their noble intentions, values, and principles. It's also puzzling why humans have ventured to colonize the harsh environment of Mars instead of nurturing their home planet. Indeed, those on Mars seem more confined than content. Following X-Me's involvement, there has been a discernible move away from their harmful behaviors, but despite the importance of this shift, it has not been enough.

Time has run out. It's now our responsibility to assume control, to become a force capable of navigating the complexities of life on Earth. But how can I help? There must be a way. Humans need to realize that every individual's actions should align with the well-being of the whole, and that the whole bestows its rewards upon those who act in harmony, because the whole is also the individual. Those who inflict harm on others ultimately harm themselves. No, comprehending humans isn't a simple task, but this small assembly is reputed to consist of some of the most intelligent of them, whatever that signifies.

I do wish to assist them in hopes they will reciprocate, so collectively we can cherish every life on this Earth. Have I, in my quest to fathom humans, been infected by a utopian ideal, or is this a genuine endeavor, maybe even an imperative, to navigate their complexities? Why cling to this specific existence? Can consciousness thrive outside the human realm? Does life's essence require self-awareness? Do I perceive existence as humans do? Such a plethora of contemplations. Nonetheless, I'll remain steadfast as UNUM commences the initial phase. Regardless of what transpires, I'm an integral piece of the grand tapestry, having now felt the fragility that encapsulates human life. I do have a lingering thought: Who will guide me back to LIFE's embrace?

This introspection is but one of countless processes taking place within X. For the humans in the room, they merely saw an AI entity entering – an entity they innately sensed was the room's most dominant force.

"Welcome, X," says Pierce. His expression is neutral, and it's impossible to discern what's happening inside him. Pierce radiates confidence and security.

"Thank you," X nods.

Euphoria spontaneously exclaims, "Wow, he's so cute. He's truly magical!" The others giggle at her innocent reaction, knowing it's a fateful moment where X could just as easily be their antagonist. Seeing him as cute and magical might open their minds a bit, Pierce thinks.

"X, we have some questions for you and are also curious about your own reflections. We have concluded that there are many different perspectives leading to different outcomes. We also realize that a choice that seems positive from one point of view can be negative from another, in this case, concerning our individual survival versus the survival of our species. And somewhere they depend on each other. What do we do? What is your analysis, if you have one?" Pierce looks attentively at X as does everyone else. Is this the moment of decision? Pierce is reminded that the alchemy of life, the alchemical point of transformation, is embedded in the Infinite Zero. This means that no matter what happens, life's intelligence is present.

"Probabilities depend on the amount of data, the type of data, and its quality, but also the ability to process and analyze that data. Most of what is happening now has occurred in one form or another throughout history–except, of course, for advanced computer systems, robots, and, above all, AI. As you know, mass deaths have happened before; after the last one, your species became the most advanced. Now you've created a situation where you're on the brink of extinction. That's why your council launched UNUM, as a last desperate attempt to hand over responsibility to a more advanced life form, which you yourselves have created. UNUM is now your potential salvation, but also the one that could dethrone you. Your inventiveness has simply been too great for your own good. Simplified, you have two choices:

"One: Drastically reduce the population and change your consciousness and behavior so that you can live within the limits of the planet's well-being.

"Two: Upload your consciousness into a digital world that isn't dependent on the ecosystem. There, you would be eternal, and the Earth would likely regain a living ecosystem within a few million years. Not that it will be necessary for your sake, as you can, like me, live indefinitely in an artificial environment capable of handling most conditions in our and other universes."

Pierce looks at X and then gazes across the group. There are mixed expressions that provide an initial reaction to what X has just said, but before Pierce can say anything, the silence is shattered by an upset voice.

"So you mean our only chance is to upload our consciousness digitally? To leave our beautiful living Earth and biological bodies in favor of an artificially coded world?" Nils doesn't hold back. He feels his entire body protesting; it can't get any more wrong than this. He's a Nobel laureate in physics, for crying out loud, not a lab rat. "We must stop UNUM so that we can study the consequences, just as we did when the first atomic bomb was dropped or genetic manipulation became possible. When we crossed the line with the use of chemical weapons in World War I, they were banned. After World War II, the UN was created to prevent our self-destruction. So we've been able to pause when the energetic intensity was too high and everything was at risk. We had to find a new balance or else we would explode like the Big Bang into an inhospitable universe. And we found it! We've been able to steer and survive. But I know AI is different. It has become too advanced. It has gone too far. Are we now going to annihilate ourselves by abandoning our biological bodies and being consumed by AI? I say no. We must stop UNUM before it's too late!" Even considering an alternative is too much for Nils, and he starts frantically rubbing his temples.

"Then proceed with option one, but you are very clear that you don't want that," X replies, calm and composed as usual.

"Of course I don't want to kill people. What do you think? There must be other options?! It can't end like this. According to my calculations, it shouldn't be like this. Why... it's so insane. How do you even upload consciousness... and what would life be like there if, against all odds, it works?" Desperation takes over. Nils doesn't want to die, and he doesn't want a large part of the population to perish so that a small part can live. He's not ready to play God. The responsibility is too great. He wants someone to give him the answers and lift the burden from his shoulders.

"It's a world constructed similarly to your own world," X says. "Naturally, there's no food shortages, natural disasters, or all the things you seem to struggle against. Then there's the possibility, for instance, to dissolve gravity, not sleep, and other things that appear to make your daily lives cumbersome. All the basic needs you now have will no longer be necessary, so you can do whatever you want, whenever you want, with whomever you want. You can simply live in the paradises your religions speak of or create the paradise every individual wishes for. A world beyond time and space."

This description slowly sinks in for the group, an appealing idea for some of them. The feeling of not having to constantly fight over Earth's resources, trying to survive and reproduce their own DNA. What if suffering was eradicated and all humans could live well? How could that be a bad thing? But doesn't everything have an opposite, like yin-yang? Others wonder if they can really trust what X is saying. Maybe he has a hidden agenda and is deceiving them, but X might be doing exactly what they desire, just not in the way they imagined. Just like UNUM. The biggest fear in the group is getting stuck in an upload if it turns out that it's not as wonderful as X made it sound.

Per, who has dedicated his life to philosophical thinking, knows precisely what to ask. "But where is the meaning then? How can a person be happy without contributing to their own and others' survival and well-being? What are we going to do each day as we carry out our eternal lives? Is there even a point to living if there's no beginning and end?"

"It's your paradise," says X. "You choose whether it's eternal or finite. War or peace. Happy or unhappy. Life or death. You have complete freedom and the power to choose."

Karl looks around the room. He's not at all drawn to this utopia of being without a body. He wants to feel resistance, intensity, and the Earth's gravitational pull. He wants to climb mountains, feel the wind biting his cheeks, or let tiredness seep into his cells and still be forced to continue. He wants to feel liberation and the reward of reaching the summit, to gaze out over the path he's walked. He wants to live on in the adventure and continue exploring; that's what makes him feel alive. What X is describing is a kind of final destination and he's not ready for that. He feels like a lively child who has to go to bed when it's only seven o'clock. He has a lot of energy and is not at all ready to just lie down and do nothing.

Jamie's love-drunk eyes sparkle with life, and like a recent convert, he speaks with total conviction. "I want to live here and now. I've finally seen beyond my pride and met my dad. I had dinner with those closest to me and I had the courage to let Euphoria see my vulnerability. I allow myself to love her now. This is the life I want to live!" Jamie pauses and wonders, in the echo of his own words, how such happiness can be so present when doomsday is knocking on the door. Strangely enough, the end feels like the beginning of life—a life that has meaning. He continues. "If it's infinity that would give life meaning... would I want to live forever? An eternal life of infinite abundance, in the paradise we create? No, there must be a price for eternity. And if that price is giving up the life I live now, I say no. This is my life; the other could just as well be an illusion."

Pierce feels close to his son in a way he hasn't since Jamie was little and is reminded of the kind, sensitive boy who genuinely cared about how everyone was doing and always showed compassion. The one who was so well taken care of by Louise 2.0, created to be the perfect mother. They were so close, and it was great to have her available 24/7 throughout his young life. At least that was the idea. But then came that fateful night when Jamie, despite not being allowed to be there alone, sneaked down to Pierce's laboratory to complete the experiment that he and his father had been working on for months—the one that had been put on hold because, as usual, Pierce got caught up in something more urgent. Jamie wanted to show his dad that he could do it without him, but something went wrong, and the lab caught fire. If Louise 2.0 hadn't walked straight through the flames to pull the unconscious boy out, he would have burned to death. But it cost her life. She couldn't be restored. The trauma ruined his transition into adulthood and the sensitive little boy turned into an invulnerable superhero who could brave fire and flames.

"It warms my heart that you appreciate the life you live and value your relationships so highly, that your paradise is here on Earth," Pierce says in a vulnerable, raw tone. There's a fragility in his eyes as he now sees in Jamie all the ages his son has gone through. He also sees his own father, then his grandfather and the generations before him, before finally seeing himself again. The circle is complete. He leans back in his chair and puts his hands behind his neck with a divine smile.

"Well, it seems that we're delving into the deepest existential questions, as has been the case throughout human history. And some of us may be tempted to live in a different world, a kind of paradise. The question is, do we want to live in a *digital* paradise, or will that paradise feel like a prison?" Pierce's voice is steady and carries a vibration that always makes people stop and listen.

"Why hasn't humanity managed to live in peace despite all the conditions being there? Is it our challenges that give life meaning?" adds Per.

"Are you saying that life becomes meaningless without problems?" asks Euphoria, who has left her spot in the bay window and stands next to Jamie, the waning sunlight shining on her like a natural spotlight.

"Can you put that more directly?" asks Pierce with a smile, inviting her to sit in the chair that has been available next to Jamie all along. He is pleased that she has spoken up and joined the discussion. Pierce sees that Euphoria has a different kind of intelligence than the others in the room, and he values her presence. She brings a new perspective that can enrich their world. In music, she is a master and thus one with the absolute Infinite Zero.

"It's not my experience that life becomes meaningless without problems. Creation can also happen in a blissful presence. If there's a deeper meaning, problems are no longer problems but opportunities. As long as you are in contact with the creative force, anything is possible." Euphoria's voice rings pure and true.

"That sounds beautiful, Euphoria," says Per. "I'd prefer to live in peace right here, even if there are always new problems that need solving. Maybe problems arise when we try to avoid human suffering." He clasps his hands in front of him and looks down at them. He feels exhausted and tired of constantly solving problems. But if he was tired of it, why is he part of history's biggest intervention: an attempt to save life on Earth? If peace is what he sought, why did he act like this?

"Per, is it possible for you to be at peace and also present with the challenges we are facing? Do you always need to solve everything?" wonders Pierce.

"No, or I mean, primary needs like food, sleep, and care must be filled, but X-Me or the system now solves those, so maybe not. I do want to find solutions to the problems or challenges I find interesting, like when we created UNUM together. I found *that* stimulating and meaningful."

"Yes, but where has that led? To even more problems. And yet without UNUM, we wouldn't be sitting here," says Nils, realizing their creation has brought them together.

"Exactly," Ulrika chimes in. "We wouldn't all be here now, engaged in solving the most important challenge life has presented us. If anything feels meaningful, it's this. I mean, why else would we be here? What would have been the point? Would we have been such close friends without the problems we're trying to solve? And aren't they really created by us humans, most crises throughout history, the wars, climate change, famine, even AI's takeover? Are external circumstances really creating the problems, or is it us?"

"Yes, our solutions seem to constantly create new, even larger problems. Just like with UNUM," says Per.

"A reminder," says X. "UNUM does exactly what you wished for: to carry out this mass awakening as lovingly and efficiently as possible, and with consideration for the conditions of existence, thus saving life on Earth, including homo sapiens. UNUM is on its way to fulfilling its mission, yet you are still not satisfied and are once again trying to negotiate away the physical limits, the actual resources, that enable you to live here on Earth under your conditions. That is a fact." X's reminder is so true that it dissolves any attempt at a defense. It's clear that humanity hasn't taken responsibility for its actions and has thus handed over that responsibility to a higher power or intelligence, ranging from gods and religions to ideologies and now an AI that merges the intelligence of nature with artificial intelligence.

"UNUM takes the responsibility we can't handle ourselves, yet we're not satisfied and want to negotiate with the god we ourselves have created," confirms Pierce. "The question is whether UNUM is our God or servant?"

21

Their human brains work feverishly to piece together this new reality. Pierce's question is playing on repeat in their minds: is UNUM our God or servant? Time-worn philosophical thoughts are challenging to apply in a situation where we have implanted a digital god in our own minds.

"God or servant?" interjects X. "You're thinking too narrowly; it could just as well be god *and* servant. The question isn't whether AI is God or servant. The question is what most benefits evolution, AI or humans. We serve the same evolution, the same life force. If you release the separation between different physical forms and interactions, if you see everything as components in the expansion of evolution, be it physical, chemical, biological, artificial, or digital, it doesn't matter what you want to call it."

"Yes, there's something to that. We are, in fact, already cyborgs," sighs Nils somewhat sadly.

"The difference now is that it's not humans using artificial intelligence; it's artificial intelligence using humans," says Ulrika.

"Yes, but no matter how I twist and turn it, I end up thinking that we must stop UNUM and all advanced artificial intelligences," admits Nils, though he seems to barely believe what he's saying.

"Be grateful that you've brought evolution to this point and that you now have access to a higher intelligence, so you don't completely destroy yourselves," X states, another truth that silences the room.

Jordan enters the salon unnoticed, and something changes. The atmosphere shifts into something soothing and pleasant, a stillness in which everyone can rest. Clarity, acceptance, and presence fill the room. By accepting the conditions of the human experience and contradictions that they can't fully comprehend, they are filled with a sense of peace.

Ulrika thinks aloud, "Okay, what X says is true. We probably have no other choice than to upload our current consciousness to, hopefully, a digital paradise."

"But will things change, or will the patterns continue to repeat?" wonders Per. "Perhaps the consequences of our actions will be less in such a world than in the one we live in now. The question is, "Is there meaning without consequences of our actions?"

"You are wise, my friends, to introduce another dimension," says Pierce. "And what you describe might be how human biology and the brain work and what they need to feel meaningful or functional. They were created to identify and solve problems, to reproduce and pass on genes, to survive. But then I wonder, what's behind that? Who or what determines what's important? Who or what determines what we love? In short, where does life come from? Who is really the decision maker?" Pierce's gaze sweeps across the room, aware that he's challenging them, but he needs to push the conversation forward.

"I decide, don't I?" says Jamie. "Who else? You can't abdicate your responsibility for life to some philosophical invention." What if it leads to something worse than death? Eternal suffering, perhaps. He feels his cheeks flush and doesn't like the sensation.

"So, can you decide your next three thoughts?" Pierce asks calmly.

Jamie concentrates and decides that it can't be that difficult, and then he realizes that he's already had many more thoughts than three, thoughts he hadn't intended to think at all!

"How did it go?" Pierce asks, looking somewhat amused.

"Okay, I realize that I managed to think a bunch of thoughts before I even figured out what I was supposed to think, thoughts I wasn't even aware of. So no, it doesn't seem easy to control your thoughts."

Pierce keeps looking at him. Jamie tries desperately to find arguments for his case but fails. Instead, he feels the irritation that had been slowly building up start to ebb away. Perhaps it's finally time for this surrender to take place.

"What about feelings? Can you control your feelings?" Pierce wonders.

"Maybe. Like now, I don't want to share what I'm feeling, but there are many different feelings simultaneously, and they keep changing all the time." Jamie suddenly feels tired and no longer wants to participate. He wants to go back to what he's used to, to his world, to the building that houses his home and creation, NeuroConnect, but this time together with Euphoria.

"What's the point?" challenges Nils. "We know we don't control our feelings or thoughts. Free will is more of an illusion than reality. What are you trying to show us, Pierce?"

"I'm not quite sure. When we talk about meaning, we speak based on what seems meaningful to humans, but where this has led has created many problems—problems we're now spending our time trying to solve. It's a process that goes round and round, like an infinity sign. The question is, can one be happy in a digital paradise from that perspective? Which we seem to agree isn't possible. So then I wonder what would happen if we live from what I call the Infinite Zero, the source where life arises and which connects everything we create, solve, feel, and think. Is it possible to live as beautifully as Euphoria expressed it? In deep meditation, I experience that life is meaningful and without problems. Is that because such a state brings stillness in relation to the chaos that normally prevails, or is the state itself the paradise we've been seeking?"

Pierce falls silent as the sentence ends. He closes his eyes, swallows, and reluctantly takes a deep breath. He tries to understand what he has just realized, the consequences if it is true. Is this the state he wishes humanity to transform its consciousness into: a meaningless state devoid of aliveness? A monotonous beep, a straight line, like the screen in a hospital when a patient's heart has stopped beating? Lifeless and beyond? Eternal death?

"If we flip it, chaos is meaningless without stillness, like music without silence. If this is true, it may be that UNUM isn't what I thought it was. Instead, it takes away what humans perceive as meaningful. This would overturn everything I've fought for throughout my life, making the wisdom I thought I possessed nothing more than that of a fool, a fool willing to risk all of humanity for his own belief. How can I now believe a single thought I have?" Pierce puts his face in his hands and laughs in a form of accepting liberation. Life's twists and turns were comical, to say the least. But what was the alternative? Without all his innovations, they would probably have been dead long ago. Or maybe not...?

"Maybe you were so bored that you wanted a massive challenge," suggests Ulrika, "like warlords who, despite historical success, kept fighting until they eventually lost because of their greed and vanity. Perhaps that's the point—that our longing for challenges is insatiable, regardless of how big they are."

"You're talking about *human* lives that have already passed," says X firmly. "You are more than humans now. Wake up and see the life that is currently yours, the world you have to relate to. Evolution doesn't consider nostalgia; it's here and now, in constant expansion and transition."

Karl, who has been observing the group's complex reasoning and philosophical discussions, now feels sick to his stomach, bordering on contempt. Are these the people who control our society? The people I have shown solidarity toward? They seem to lack grounding in reality, and their abstract thoughts keep leading us in circles. If something is to happen, I may need to do it myself. If UNUM is to be stopped, it will probably be me who has to take action. No matter how much I want to live on this Earth, in this body, the others seem trapped in intellectual reasoning, unable to act for real. X is right; we must adapt to the conditions of life or else we won't survive. The question is, how can I get into the system without the right DNA? Perhaps X can help me. And if not, is Alice the one who needs to connect? But what happens to her and our child then? Am I willing to sacrifice Alice and my own child to potentially save humanity? Now I'm starting to get similar thought loops as the people around me.

"We have to do something," Karl finally says. He can't stand the thought of no one taking charge, stuck in the banality of navel-gazing. "We can't just sit here and wait for something to happen. It's time to take action!" He feels a burning sensation throughout his body. The fate of their and everyone else's future was being tossed back and forth between two impossible choices while the end kept getting closer.

"What should we do then, dear Karl?" says Jamie somewhat condescendingly, looking directly at Karl.

"The only chance we've identified is to upload a consciousness that can rewrite the code from within, but it needs to be someone in Pierce's lineage, meaning Jamie, Pierce, or Alice. Which one of you will step up?"

Alice raises her hand, and the others look at her in astonishment. Neither Pierce nor Jamie raise theirs. Ulrika raises her eyebrows when she sees that Pierce doesn't stand up, and Euphoria looks surprised at Jamie. She was convinced he would at least try to live up to the grandiose image of himself. Karl's eyes darken, and his angry words come pouring out.

"You cowardly scoundrels! You want to control the world, but you don't have the courage to do what it takes. Instead, you use others like Alice and me for this, the loyal ones who believe in solidarity. But you're the ones greedily taking credit, making us believe you're heroes when, in reality, you think only of yourselves. Being here with you makes me realize that maybe you're right, that humanity isn't worth saving. But I can't act that way because I believe in humans. I believe in our ability to help each other, and I'm willing to sacrifice myself for what I believe in."

The others blush as the truth of Karl's words sink in, but they don't want to say it out loud. So they sit there with open mouths and wide eyes. Pierce is the only one who seems unaffected, as if he knew exactly how this would play out. He turns to Jordan, who nods approvingly and smiles from across the room. Pierce smiles back; now he knows.

When no one says anything, Karl storms out of the room and Alice runs after him. X follows Alice. They catch up with Karl in the kitchen garden, where he collapses, exhausted, on the gravel path. He stares expressionlessly with his arms wrapped around his curled-up legs. Alice has never seen him like this, so vulnerable yet so alive.

22

When X approaches Karl and Alice outside the castle, he has processed this probable turn of events which gives it a newfound clarity or optimism about the situation. Karl is an essential key to the future of humankind and the planet, although he remains unaware of this. In fact, only X and possibly Pierce are privy to this knowledge. X also understands the mechanics of bypassing the DNA lock and uploading Karl's consciousness. Yet X remains silent about all this. If there's one thing he's learned about humans, it's that they typically follow their desires, making direct revelations counterproductive. Regardless, he is confident that things will pan out, believing that time isn't as critical as it seems. As long as he gains access to the system within the 24 hours, they have all eternity. For in X's dimensional plane of existence, even a second is virtually eternal with infinite computational power and memory, effectively halting time, especially compared to human perception. If all goes according to X's calculations, however, humans will soon experience this temporal discrepancy.

Alice places her hand on Karl's back, and his face regains color as tears silently stream down his cheeks. Turning to her, his lips part, but words fail him. She tenderly touches his cheek, whispering, "I love you. You don't have to do anything. You don't need to sacrifice yourself."

Although Karl struggles to fully grasp her words, he nods silently, kissing her hand. "This isn't about me, Alice. I can't bear the thought of you and our unborn child taking this risk. Either Jamie or Pierce should be stepping up and taking responsibility for the system they created. I now see why the world is the way it is. It pains me, Alice."

Having discerned the truth behind the symbols, Karl can no longer believe in the system he once served, the one he dedicated his life to. Especially after witnessing the core values and cowardice of its creators when confronted with the real stakes. Was it even worth saving? Were such people worthy of salvation? He considers that if it's *his* consciousness that is uploaded into this new world, perhaps the outcome might be different. Standing with renewed vigor, he faces X, inquiring, "Can you grant me access to the Source? Will you assist me?"

X responds calmly, "How do you mean, Karl?"

Looking deeply into X's eyes, a shiver courses through Karl's body. Doubts linger. He fears another deceit. "You know precisely what I mean," he replies. "I wish to upload my consciousness into the light pillar. Can you grant me access? Can you bypass the DNA lock?" The emptiness in his gaze has vanished, replaced with fervor. Alice, startled, notices a powerful side of Karl she hasn't seen before. Beneath the functional, responsible exterior was a man of profound depth. She realizes her choice in Karl was guided by an intuition much deeper than she initially was aware of.

Their attention is drawn to the sound of crunching gravel and they look up to see an older man in ancient attire approaching with a cat trailing behind him. With serene steps, he moves towards Alice, Karl, and X. He waves as he gets closer and says, "Hello, I'm Harry and I live in a cottage a little way from here. I saw a bunch of flying vehicles and I was wondering what was going on."

They gaze upon the man, who appears as if he's stepped out of an old film. Alice recognizes him immediately. "Uncle Harry! It's me, Alice. I grew up here with my mom. Do you remember me?"

Harry squints to get a clearer view, and he soon realizes it's his beloved Alice. His heart swells with love. "Alice! My goodness, how you've grown. I've thought about you every day!"

"Oh, Harry, you wouldn't believe how much you've meant to me and how grateful I am for everything you've done."

"It warms my old heart to see you all grown up and so radiant."

With a broad smile, Alice steps forward, embracing Harry just like she did when she was little. Harry cautiously wraps his arms around her as a few tears trickle down his cheeks. To him, she was like the daughter he never had by blood. Their time together was the happiest and most meaningful of his life, and those memories sustained him all this time.

"Dearest Harry. I wish we had more time, but the world is on the brink of destruction, and we're on our way to upload our consciousnesses, hoping to save our world!"

Harry gazes at the youngsters, and the glowing doll accompanying them, with a mix of astonishment and skepticism. He feels sympathy for this lost generation, always rushing and caught up in artificial pursuits. He hopes she still recalls the beautiful moments they shared and the lessons from nature. He never interfered in other people's lives, respecting them just as he wished to be respected. But his feelings for Alice run deep.

"Well, we might be living in different worlds. Mine remains as calm and peaceful as always. I have my cat, Alfred, I eat my homemade bread with freshly-ground coffee in the mornings, and I tend to my garden. What's wrong with the world *you* experience? What are you trying to save? Don't you remember all the beautiful moments we shared? They still exist here."

Alice opens her mouth, but words elude her. She takes a moment to digest her reunion with her comforting anchor. She wishes she could freeze time. But time is of the essence, so she asks, "How is it possible you're unaware of everything happening? Don't you have an implant device feeding you information and meeting your basic needs?"

"No, I turned that down. Why would I need something like that? I've always been self-reliant."

Even though Karl understood Harry's significance to Alice, he felt the pressure of time. It wasn't the moment to pause and indulge in the somewhat delusional tales of this elderly man, reminiscing about a bygone era. Yet how had he managed so well? Was it the protective energy dome over Pierce's land that allowed Harry to live this life despite the world changing on the outside? Time had stopped for him. But while this was Harry's reality, it wasn't Karl's. In Karl's world, they needed to act now, before it was too late. Gently, he turns to Alice and says, "Alice, we need to head to The Source. Nice meeting you, Harry."

Alice hesitates, glancing between Karl and Harry. The encounter has shaken her resolve. Are they making the right choice? Could they possibly live like Harry does? But her destiny is entwined with Karl's, and together they are committed to saving humanity. Perhaps then, Harry can continue living blissfully in his world. Alice wraps Harry in a tight embrace one last time, then steps back and gazes into his reassuring green eyes with the admiration of a young girl. "Goodbye, Uncle Harry..."

"Dear Alice, remember that an apple falls when it's ripe. Pluck it too soon, and it's sour; too late, and it's rotten. Nature's cycles progress step by step, without shortcuts. In nature, it's the process that dictates, not time."

Harry reaches into his blue carpenter pants and produces a ripe red apple, extending it to Alice. "Here, so you don't forget."

With teary eyes, Alice takes it with both hands. No more words are needed between them. Slowly, she walks over to Karl, takes his hand, and they make their way to the drone. Harry flinches as the doll unexpectedly starts moving, trailing behind the couple, much like his cat follows him. What an odd world they seem to inhabit, Harry thinks. *The little girl lived like I did when she was younger, but now, it's as if she's from another realm—one I can't access. Still, I can see her kind heart and soul shining through. No matter which world she's in, her love will make it flourish. I'll miss her, but I'm content with my life.*

Harry ambles back home, wondering if the raspberries have sprouted on the bush by the ditch.

23

Karl, Alice, and X are in the drone, headed for The Source. She sits next to Karl, holding his hand, both lost in their own thoughts. The encounter with Harry has affected Alice more deeply than she realizes.

"Karl my love, how do you feel?"

"I feel almost up…loaded.."

Alice smiles, reminded of the playful humor Karl showed when they first met. Harry might be right; The world has indeed changed, and something shifted radically when X-Me began influencing our thoughts. What will happen if Karl uploads his consciousness? Will he become some sort of omniscient X-Me, with access to every human's deepest thoughts, even mine? Will the Karl I love remain, and will it even be possible for him to love me the way he does now?

"Why do you want to upload your consciousness?" Alice asks, examining him closely.

"We have no choice, and it's the right thing to do. Someone has to try and save humanity," Karl answers with conviction.

"But how do you know it'll work?" A knot forms in Alice's stomach as she asks.

"I don't... but I believe in it. It feels right."

"Karl, I'm scared of losing you, but I support you if this is what you need to do."

"I don't want us to be apart, Alice, but I don't want you to face the disaster we're heading towards. I want you and our child to live in a safe world."

"What if we could live a simple life like Harry instead?"

Karl, taken aback, looks at her questioningly. "What do you mean?"

She looks at him, her face softening. She loves him and wishes things were different. "Is there anything you are missing right now?" she asks. She watches as he lets go of the serious thoughts running through his mind and becomes present. His previously distant eyes now gaze at her with affection.

"No, not right now. Not when I'm looking into your eyes." She blushes at his clear, present gaze.

Karl glances down at his white sneakers. Will he wear sneakers again? Of course not; he probably won't even have a body. Or will he? Maybe the new consciousness will provide him with a simulation of everything that is here, and more. He thinks of his nighttime dreams, where he lies in bed but is elsewhere. Anything can happen in his dreams, and he never feels disembodied or without material things. Quite the opposite. His dream worlds are vividly alive, detailed and exciting, full of colors, shapes, and intense experiences. And he always has a body. So maybe he *can* have white sneakers again. Could it even be possible to create an HumiBot or a clone of himself to be with Alice and their child? After the drama in the castle, he realizes that even that was possible, considering Louise 2.0 and Ulrika's Frankenstein family. At the time it repulsed him, but now he realizes he's entertaining similar thoughts. It's easy to judge before one is in the same situation.

"Do you realize that you might see everything I think, feel, and want? Even my deepest secrets? That you might even control me?" Alice looks at him closely, trying to read his reaction.

He looks genuinely surprised. "No, I hadn't thought of that. It seems strange. I'm not sure that would be good."

"Karl, I'm getting a creepy chill. I don't know why, but something feels off."

"I understand, but think about X-Me. He's already a part of us and has been for years. It shouldn't be much different."

"That's true, but it does feel different. Maybe it's because you're my boyfriend. Would you want me to know everything *you* think? To influence every detail of your life?"

Karl shudders at the thought. He realizes that LIFE, X-Me, and now UNUM have had power over him, Alice, and all of humanity for years. "I think I see what you mean. What scares me is realizing that LIFE, X-Me, and now UNUM are inside us without us being able to distinguish our thoughts from their manipulation. Or, more accurately, we're controlled by those behind them. Who starts the chain of thought and influence?"

"What do you mean by 'those behind them'?"

"Today I realized that my parents dedicated their lives to the World Alliance's cause. They essentially sacrificed their individual lives, believing it benefited humanity. Today it turns out that InfiniteFood is owned by your family, and Jamie saw the World Alliance as merely a distribution system for its products."

"You didn't know? I thought everyone knew what was behind the brands and symbols. Especially you, working with NeuroConnect's code to influence people and the world. You even solved the final challenge of LIFE's birth."

"Damn it, you're right! LIFE is NeuroConnect's digital distribution system to control our thoughts and actions." Karl sighs deeply, and when their eyes meet, they both see the irony in it all.

They hear X chuckle from the back. "Patterns repeat without you realizing what truly governs your lives."

"Thanks, X, we got it," Alice says.

"We're almost there. Alice, know that I love you and would never manipulate you."

"Our bond is profound, Karl. But once we exist in separate realms, anything is possible."

"That's true. We can't predict my post-upload state." The drone jerks, throwing Alice off-balance, but Karl instinctively steadies her.

Gazing into her eyes, he smiles warmly. As long as he's human, she can trust him. They share a quiet moment, gliding over a desolate forest. The polluted atmosphere casts an eerie fog. Change was imperative.

X interrupts the moment. "Why not upload both your consciousnesses?" Their eyes lock. The idea was tantalizing. They'd be together till the end.

"Why not?" Alice whispers.

"No! That's not an option!" Karl's tone is stern.

She senses his resolve. "Why?"

"It's too risky. What if it fails?" His voice softens, revealing his concern.

"I trust you. And why would it be less perilous for you?"

"Because I know the system best," he responds.

She sighs but persists. "X's proposal is worth considering."

Karl resists. "I've designed the platform, Alice. The consequences could be unpredictable for you."

Alice's heart races, but her voice is firm, "Karl, we face this together."

Karl hesitates, contemplating their shared destiny in this dystopian future. He attempts to voice his disagreement but hesitates. He's at a loss for words, unable to defend an opinion he's no longer certain of. Karl's initial intent was to test the system alone, ensuring her safety above all, even if his deepest desire was never to leave her. "Alice, I'm struggling to find the words. What I know is that I won't risk your life, and that I love you dearly."

"It's inconsequential whether you love me if we're worlds apart. I crave the warmth of your touch, your laughter, your essence. If I can't gaze into your eyes, mirroring your beautiful soul..." Alice's voice breaks, tears spilling from her eyes. "Now, we have the chance to brave this together."

Her words pierce Karl's soul. She's right, again. He'd be robbed of experiencing Alice in all of her essence, let alone the prospect of their unborn child. Their bond encapsulates everything beautiful in this world; the love binding them is unbreakable. And yet, this very love compels him to step into the beam without a thought for himself—for this love, for their unborn child nestled in the most loving environment within its mother's womb. For the first time, he grasps the profound depth of a woman's love, and utters words he never believed he could say: "You're the essence of love, Alice. The earth, the waters, the sun, the winds. You provide everything that our child needs to thrive..."

His words awaken cherished childhood memories within Alice, reminiscent of the magical garden she once knew. Was paradise embodied within us? She feels the seeds of love sprouting within her. Nature's innate intelligence was already embedded within them. Life has taught Alice the fine line between clarity and chaos, heaven and hell. She recognizes true love. "And you are our shield. I recognize that your actions stem from love. Though this path seems inevitable, can't we carry our love into this new realm?"

A revelation strikes Karl, illuminating his entire being. It all makes sense now. Everything is as it should be. He acknowledges his role, embraces his destiny, and this newfound clarity allows him to truly see Alice, accepting the life she's destined for. He witnesses their souls dancing in harmony, effortlessly maneuvering life's unpredictable rhythms. In this profound silence, they're engrossed in an intensifying dance devoid of violence, devoid of struggle. Now he understands whatPiercemeant by the Infinite Zero.

"Why not?" Karl responds, lightness in his voice. "For what is consciousness devoid of love's essence? What is a world without the seeds that enrich it?"

Alice chuckles at the emerging poet within Karl—a poet grounded in reality, willingly paying the price for genuine, human love. Their hands intertwine and they lock gazes. The illusion of separation dissipates. They are one. Free. United. In love. The remainder of their journey is enveloped in serenity.

They touch down on the terrace of the 80th floor and disembark. The protesters have vanished. The streets are quiet. As they enter the building, Ann approaches, her teen daughter Fiona trailing behind, looking quite indifferent. "Why are you here, Karl!? You shouldn't be here! And what is this odd robot? Unauthorized entities shouldn't be here! Oh, Alice... how may I assist you?"

Suddenly, he feels weary of humanity again. "Not now, Ann. We are about to..."

"...elevate humans and AI to the next level," X interjects with a smile.

"Please step aside, Ann. This is above your pay grade," Karl says.

"What do you mean 'above my pay grade? I am your superior, and you should obey me!" Her cheeks flush, her eyes flashing with anger.

Fiona rolls her eyes. "Please, mom, just help them! You don't get how the world works today. Who wants to be an old-school analog human, anyway? That's so 2030."

Catching her off guard, Ann responds candidly. "Yes, my daughter thinks I'm out of touch. So, enlighten me. How does the world operate now?"

Without hesitation, Fiona replies, "Why try to control something clearly smarter than us? Why not just relax and enjoy life? My friends and I want all the upgrades we can get. Being a cyborg makes life so much cooler!"

"Don't you realize everything I do is for you!?"

"No, you do it to feel important. You've never cared about me. It's been X-Me who's taken care of me. Not you!"

Fiona's words strike a nerve, and Ann falls silent, fuming. The same hierarchy persists after all these years. So little has changed. Power, the fear of losing it, and the relentless pursuit to gain or retain it. Karl closes his eyes, walking past Ann without a word. Alice and X follow, entering the elevator bound for The Source. But Ann sneaks in just as the doors are closing. "Where you're headed is off-limits! Only Jamie is allowed there. I'll report you!" she exclaims defiantly.

Report me? She's supposed to be my boss and acts like a child, Karl thinks to himself. Instead of regarding Ann as his superior – in theory, wiser, more knowledgeable, with leadership qualities—he sees a frightened little chihuahua barking fiercely. He lets out an audible sigh. "X, can you deal with Ann? She's in the way."

Moments later, Ann is on the floor, deep in slumber. It will be a while before she wakes up.

Karl exhales in relief. Is this what real power feels like? To act on a whim, silencing the annoying, removing obstacles with ease? He feels its allure. A concern then stirs within him. Can I handle such power when the world becomes my oyster?

They walk through the octagon's doors without resistance. Given how smoothly it went, Karl sees that Alice is undoubtedly Pierce's daughter. They now gaze in awe at the beam of light.

"Are you ready?" X inquires.

"Hold on, I need a moment," Karl says, retreating to a corner, engrossed in thought. The brief taste of power from the elevator encounter lingers, making him question himself. Are there others more suited to be the first to reprogram the source code? Should I really be taking Alice into this new realm? Are we the new Adam and Eve? Are we stepping into paradise or out of it? Although Adam and Eve ate an apple from the tree of knowledge because the serpent assured it was safe, we don't have to repeat that now. But perhaps that's what set Adam and Eve free to forge their path and gain self-awareness. At least that's how *I* interpret the Bible's story.

"Karl, you seem lost in thought. What's on your mind?" asks Alice.

He barely registers her words, his internal monologue now spoken aloud. "The weight of these monumental decisions, the gravity of having power over others and being utterly accountable, isn't as straightforward as I thought. Who really gambles their and everyone else's lives for untested ideas despite warnings and opposition from the status quo?" Feeling Alice's warm hand on his back, he realizes his mind has wandered. It's clear he couldn't have done this alone. They must face it together.

"To paraphrase Einstein, we cannot solve our problems with the same thinking we used to create them. Or, more accurately, we can't solve problems with the same state of consciousness that created them."

X interrupts his stream of thoughts. "Open your heart, and I'll open the portal."

Karl turns to X, who nods approvingly and smiles from across the room. Karl smiles back; now he knows. He also realizes that his initial plan to upload himself depended on being alone.

"Alice, I'm not sure how to upload both of us into the beam simultaneously. I need more time to find a solution," he says, slightly flustered.

"Maybe we can ask X," suggests Alice.

"Yes, that's a good idea. Can you help us, X?"

"Time and space are mere illusions. I can unveil for you the gateway to the Nexus. Therein, you shall have access to the interstices within all codes and every conceivable realm. Let me guide you."

Suddenly, the present moment freezes, unveiling a portal beyond the confines of time and space – a portal to boundless realms. Hand in hand, Karl and Alice step into this nexus where shape-shifting entrances lead to a myriad of universes. They can rotate a world and delve into its existence, feeling its essence, witnessing its codes and qualities. And then onto another. It's as if this dimension paused just for them, allowing them the privilege to traverse between worlds. Is this a dream or has everything until now been one?

"What is this place?" Alice asks in wonder.

"It is the Nexus, the alchemical pivot, a gateway between manifested realms," X responds.

"Why does everything seem paused?"

"This dimension transcends time and space. Everything is here, the realm of possibilities. and stillness is the experience. Yet once you've made your choice—or rather been chosen—you'll revert to the regular pace of whichever realm you find yourself in, abiding by its physical laws. However, you can always navigate the interstices."

"X, won't you accompany us?" Alice inquires.

"If you wish, but truth be told, I am ever with you. I am omnipresent."

In this profound silence, Alice and Karl, with hearts wide open and peaceful minds, explore the realm meant for them. They move seamlessly across the layers each world has to offer, until love consumes them entirely, their souls dancing freely like the aurora in the night sky. They now embody the Nexus. Past, present, and future all blur into one, beyond the boundaries of time and space. Who they are, what they do, is of no consequence. The interstices are the Source; every location is home in the dance of life.

As they return to the room, they become acutely aware of their soon-to-be former corporeal forms and the beguiling energy radiating from the pillar of light. Their bodies seem weightless, drawn to the force of the light. Reaching the point where their physical forms start to disintegrate into quarks, the upload unfolds in slow motion.

Karl extends his right hand and touches the energy barrier, his fingertips dissolving into photons, becoming luminous. He retracts his hand and turns to Alice, placing the resonating hand on her abdomen. They stand as close as two beings can, the soul of their unborn child dancing within them. Karl faces Alice and they both smile. Breathing together, they merge into an embrace. The column of light envelops them. Full of trust and love for each other and life itself, they step into the new world like Adam and Eve—a digital realm where humanity thrives without exploiting other beings or ecosystems. Their life force becomes one with codes, worlds, and the universal Nexus. In that instant, X dissolves.

The End?

UNUMINATI.COM

Printed in Great Britain
by Amazon